"I was disappointed— at first."

"And then?" nothing more

She shrugged. I don't think it pays to take these things too seriously."

"What things?"

She looked at him, but kept her distance, trying not to feel the attraction that made her long to reach out to him. "I guess I mean...things between men and women who are so different."

"Are we so different? I didn't think so the other night." His blue eyes were soft with appeal.

Rennie's resolve wavered. She'd never wanted anything as much as she wanted to walk into his arms that minute. But how could she, knowing that she would always come second?

"Connor, please. It isn't going to work out for us."

A muscle in his cheek moved. For a long moment he studied her face as if memorizing every feature. Then quietly he turned and left her alone.

Amanda Clark is the pseudonym for the mother-daughter writing team of Janet O'Daniel and Amy Midgley. They began collaborating on romances long-distance, when they lived in different states. Now they've both moved to South Carolina, which makes working together a lot less complicated. Janet and Amy have extensive writing backgrounds, including fiction, nonfiction and newspaper journalism. This is their fourth book for Harlequin Romance.

Books by Amanda Clark

EARLY HARVEST
Amanda Clark

Harlequin Books

TORONTO • NEW YORK • LONDON
AMSTERDAM • PARIS • SYDNEY • HAMBURG
STOCKHOLM • ATHENS • TOKYO • MILAN
MADRID • WARSAW • BUDAPEST • AUCKLAND

ISBN 0-373-03321-4

EARLY HARVEST

Copyright © 1994 by Amanda Clark.

CHAPTER ONE

RENNIE SURVEYED the group standing in front of her. Seven. Eight, if you included Pete, the little corgi sitting alertly at her feet. Not bad for the first day. But more would come later, she reassured herself. All the kids had seemed excited about the project when she'd discussed it with them on the last day of school.

"Okay, everyone, listen up," she said, even though she knew they were already listening. Staring at her glumly, in fact, and waiting for her to explain to them how this rubble-strewn patch of rock-hard city ground could ever be made to bloom and blossom. "Today we have to do a little cleanup job."

"You said we were going to plant stuff." Teddy Pohl sounded accusing. Small and pale and thin, he stood there in stiff new jeans, clutching a paper cup with something growing in it.

"We are, Teddy. Only first we have to get the ground ready for planting. That's what real farmers do."

Seven pairs of eyes looked at her accusingly. "How are we going to do that?" Becky Harmon demanded. She was stocky and scowling, arms folded in front of her, red hair blazing, and she had a ten-year-old's endless store of questions, as Rennie well knew.

"First we have to clean up all this junk." For a brief moment Rennie's eyes swept over the vista of broken bottles, old tires, beer cans, fast-food wrappers and plastic shopping bags. The lot was bordered by a gas station on one side, and on the other by a deserted factory building where workmen were loudly doing renovations. "After that we add manure and plow it into the soil with a tractor."

One of the boys shouted, "Pew!" and held his nose; others followed suit. Rennie ignored them. "I've brought containers for the trash. We'll load them onto the truck when they're full, to go to the dump and the recycling center. Everyone have work gloves? Don't pick up anything with your bare hands. How about sunscreen? I have some we can share."

To set an example she brought out the tube and began coating her own face and arms. Sun was a powerful presence in this South Carolina coastal city. From the gas station next door came a hissing sound as someone began putting air in his tires. To Rennie it sounded discouragingly like a comment on the whole project. She tamped down the thought firmly and went on.

"Randolph, did you bring gloves for your little brother?" She didn't ask why he'd brought the six-year-old along. She knew Randolph must be in charge of him this summer while their mother was at work. And she was pretty sure both kids had been coerced into coming. She could picture Mrs. Simms, a hard-working black woman worried about her boys, saying, "You go help the teacher with that garden, you hear? You stay offa them streets."

"Yeah, I brought 'em." Randolph exuded boredom.

"What's his name?" Rennie passed the sunscreen to Becky.

"Donald."

"Okay, Donald. I know you'll be a big help. Now let's get started. Keep everything separate. Glass in one container, plastic in another—you all know how. We'll have this place cleaned up in no time."

"What'll I do with my bean?" Teddy Pohl demanded. "I was gonna plant it."

Rennie took a deep breath. "I'll take care of it, Teddy. We may not get around to planting for a day or two."

"It's called Green Wonder," he said proudly. "I grew it from a seed."

"I'm sure it'll do well once we get the soil ready for it," she assured him. "All right, let's see how fast we can get this garbage picked up."

The job was accomplished in less time than Rennie had dared to hope, and at midday the overflowing containers were loaded into her dented pickup, ready for the dump or for recycling. Pete had long since retired from the action and allowed himself to be boosted onto the seat of the truck where he was now sleeping.

"That's wonderful! You all did beautifully," she told the kids. "Now, will everybody be back here same time tomorrow?" Her short dark hair was plastered down damply, and in spite of the sunscreen she'd used, her face was hot and prickly.

The seven heads nodded. Teddy Pohl asked, "What about this afternoon?"

Rennie hesitated. "I told your folks you'd only be working here half a day. And Randolph, your little brother may need a nap."

"I'd better take my bean home," Teddy said.

Worries crowded in on her after the children had left. All of them lived in the immediate neighborhood, she knew. They'd be fine. They were tough kids. They were used to being on their own. But if there was no one at home waiting for them, what kind of lunches would they have? And what would they do for the rest of the afternoon? Maybe she should keep them a little longer each day. If they brought sandwiches— Rennie gave her head a small shake. One thing at a time, she thought as she swung up into the truck beside Pete. She backed carefully out of the lot and headed for the town dump.

When she returned she had a hamburger at the diner across the street, splashed cold water on her face in the ladies' room and returned to the vacant lot. She admired what they'd accomplished, trying not to feel discouraged at the prospect of the vast job ahead. Her friend Sandy, who with her husband ran a boarding stable outside of town, had promised to lend her a tractor for the next day; they would also bring the manure.

Rennie's gaze, moving over the lot, came to rest on a ragged pile of lumber discarded carelessly at one side by workmen from the old building next door. The men were standing around finishing their lunches. Fast-food cartons and soft-drink cans joined the heap right where Rennie and the children had so painstakingly picked up every bit of debris that morning.

A red cloud of anger swept over Rennie. She strode across the empty lot toward the men, most of whom were drifting back inside to resume work.

"Who's in charge of this job?" she demanded.

Heads turned and admiring glances swept over her. There were one or two whistles. A tall man who'd been standing at the entrance to the building took a step forward and regarded her with obvious annoyance in his sky-blue eyes. His unruly light hair had a sun-bleached look and his rugged features reflected outdoor living. The sleeves of his denim shirt appeared to have been hacked off carelessly at the shoulder, and his jeans were faded and worn. Rennie was suddenly aware of her own grimy cutoffs and her over-the-ankle work shoes. The red bandanna around her forehead was damp with sweat.

"What's the trouble?" he said curtly, putting on the hard hat he'd been holding.

"This!" Rennie said, fury carrying her along like a wave. She stabbed a finger at the pile of debris. "Didn't you and your men see us working all morning to get this lot cleaned up? The children and I spent hours at it, and now look at this mess!"

His eyes flickered to her soiled T-shirt, which had East Side Elementary emblazoned across it.

"We were planning to clear it away at the end of the day," he said.

"That's not good enough!" she stormed. "All right, maybe today it doesn't matter, but we're making a garden here. Suppose we had things planted—seedlings and young plants. You can't get in the habit of just tossing all your refuse over here. Mr. Connor Blackstone owns this property, and he gave us permission to use it this summer. I'm sorry if it inconveniences you, but this kind of thing has to stop. *Right now.*"

The tall man was frowning at her, but the other men were obviously enjoying the scene. Someone snickered.

"And if you don't like it, too bad," Rennie went on. "I'll just have to speak to Mr. Blackstone about it. He's very sympathetic to our project."

"Is he?" A small grimace moved his mouth, then subsided.

"Well, actually he's going to build some idiot parking garage here in the fall, but he said it'll be after the growing season ends. He certainly won't be happy when I tell him about this."

"I see. An idiot parking garage."

"So will you please see to it that this junk is removed immediately?"

"We'll get to it," he said sharply, and turned away.

Helpless with anger, Rennie watched him go, then strode off herself.

When she arrived the next morning, the pile had been cleared away.

The Kenyons, Sandy and Bob, arrived early with truckloads of manure and a small tractor on a flatbed. While the two of them spread the good rich dressing over the lot, Rennie followed with the tractor, turning the soil over, going round and round until the starved city ground began to take on the look of a country field. All the children had returned to admire and cheer from the sidelines. She could tell they were yearning to drive the tractor, but she knew that she had to be sensible about possible injuries and liability, so she settled for allowing each of them to sit on the tractor seat once she'd shut off the engine.

"It smells great!" Teddy Pohl exclaimed. Rennie wasn't sure if he meant the tractor, which actually smelled of gasoline and grease, or the field itself, which suddenly and miraculously had taken on a clean springtime fragrance.

"Is it done now?" practical Becky inquired.

"Not yet. Mr. and Mrs. Kenyon have gone back for another load of dressing, and I still have more plowing to do. We'll finish up this afternoon."

"Can we come back and watch?"

Rennie hesitated. "If you'll be very good and stay out of the way, I guess you can. And you can keep an eye on Pete, so he doesn't get underfoot."

She saw them off and then glanced in the direction of the old building next door. A trash can had been placed in a conspicuous spot. Her eyes skimmed over the men, who were strolling outside to have lunch again in the early-June sunshine. There was no sign of the tall blond man who'd been so curt with her the day before. She guessed he must be the job foreman, or maybe even the architect, since his look had turned so sour when she'd slighted the prospective parking garage.

Rennie, who never ceased hoping for miracles, clung to the notion that once Connor Blackstone saw the garden, bursting with flowers and vegetables, he'd alter his plans for the garage and tell them the garden should stay permanently. Then they could put in perennials and fruit trees and gravel paths, and it would become a real oasis in this blighted worn-out part of the city.

Reality hit her like a cold shower as she recalled the yards of red tape they'd had to cut through to get even this far. Fred Swanson, the principal of her school, had listened to Rennie's pleading and had gone first to the board of education, then to the mayor's office to try to get the project off the ground. Mayor Wisner had finally agreed to intercede on their behalf with the big developer, Connor Blackstone, for the use of the lot on South Street. It was in a run-down section of the city that the mayor liked to refer to optimistically as "ripe for renewal." Both Rennie and Fred Swanson were sure the upcoming election had played a part in the mayor's cooperation. Blackstone's permission had been grudging and hedged with conditions. They could use the lot only until he was ready to start construction of the parking garage. They were not to trespass on the construction site, where the old building, once a big commercial bakery, was being remodeled into a condominium complex. He wanted no trouble with kids dashing around and becoming nuisances.

"Sounds like a real congenial type," Rennie had grumbled to Fred. "Probably kicks his dog."

"Too rich to have a dog." Fred had grinned cheerfully. "But let's not complain. You got the lot for your garden, didn't you?"

And that, Rennie supposed as she swung back into the tractor seat, was something to be grateful for. Sufficient unto the day.

By midafternoon Sandy and Bob Kenyon had returned with another load of manure.

Rennie checked on Pete's whereabouts, spotted him, then as an afterthought clipped a leash onto his collar and handed it to Becky, who, along with the other children, was watching from the sidewalk. Several passersby were also lingering with interest, and the whole scene was taking on a lively holiday appearance.

"All set!" Rennie signaled to Bob, and his big truck bumped up over the curb and into the lot. There was a scattering of cheers from the sidewalk.

"I'm cooking you two a very special dinner once this job's done," Rennie promised as she headed toward the tractor.

"We'll count on it!" Bob shouted back.

The afternoon shadows were lengthening by the time the Kenyons finished and backed their truck out. Rennie paused in her plowing long enough to wave her thanks and to check on the children and Pete. The sixth graders were still mesmerized by the tractor, Pete had fallen asleep at Becky's feet, and the group of onlookers was growing. Most of them seemed to be older men—no doubt retired—Rennie thought, but there were a few women as well.

"Almost done!" she called out to the children, who responded with waves.

But before she could turn the tractor around and resume plowing, a thin gray cat, city-grimed and wild-looking, came streaking out of nowhere and ran across the lot in the direction of the old bakery building. Pete, awakened from his nap by some ancient instinct, gave a loud bark and tore off in pursuit, leash yanked from Becky's hand and trailing after him. Then a delivery truck, loaded with lumber, turned into the paved lane where the tractor was. With the tractor blocking the way, the truck stopped, half on the street. At that moment, the tractor stalled. Rennie jumped from the seat, yelling for Pete, and all seven children came dashing out onto the lot shouting for the dog.

The truck driver, a massive burly man, swung down from his cab.

"Hey, lady, can you move that thing? I got to bring this lumber in."

Rennie, sprinting after Pete, caught up with him at the old building, where several workmen had managed to waylay him. The cat had disappeared.

"Here you go, ma'am," said one of the men, grinning broadly. "He's pretty fast for a guy with such short legs, ain't he?"

"Thank you," Rennie said, snatching the dog up in her arms and trying not to sound grudging in the face of their obvious amusement.

"Hey, lady—" the truck driver said again.

"Yes, all right, I'll move it," Rennie said through clenched teeth. "Is this the place where you always make deliveries?" She motioned with her head toward the narrow strip between the empty lot and the building.

"Gotta make 'em someplace, ain't I?"

"I just wondered. I'll have to allow for that in laying out the garden."

"You do that, ma'am," the big man said wearily. "Now would you just get that tractor outa my way? Things are starting to back up out there."

Rennie could hear impatient horns of cars held up by the huge truck, which was blocking one lane.

She put Pete down and handed his leash to Randolph. Outraged, Becky protested, "I can take care of him! He just surprised me, that's all—jumping up like that."

"Yes, of course you can, Becky," Rennie said soothingly. "But I just thought Randolph might like a turn. And, Randolph, watch out for Donald. Get him back on the sidewalk. Go on, kids. Everybody stay out of the way."

"Lady—" the truck driver said.

"All *right!* I'll be out of here in a second."

Rennie hopped back on the tractor and turned the key. The tractor refused to start. She tried again. No reaction.

In spite of her bandanna, sweat was trickling into Rennie's eyes. Her hair was flattened damply against her head. She was aware of the amusement in the faces of the men who were lined up staring at her and was beginning to feel nervous about the ominous expression on the truck driver's face.

"What's going on here?"

Rennie whirled around at the sound of the voice and found herself staring into the same sky-blue eyes she'd confronted the day before. Only today the unruly hair was brushed into a semblance of order, and instead of a denim shirt and jeans, the man was wearing a gray suit, a smooth white shirt and a tie that was definitely silk. The look on his face was the same, however. Tight-lipped, frowning, annoyed.

"What seems to be the problem?"

"Can't get my truck in," the driver said. "She's blocking my way."

"Well, move that thing, won't you?" He jerked his head at the tractor and gave Rennie an exasperated look.

"I'm trying to!" Rennie snapped. "It won't start."

Sensing an interesting situation, the seven children and Pete edged closer. Out of the corner of her eye, Rennie saw a long dark limousine parked across the street. And to make matters worse, a policeman was bearing down on the scene.

"You'll have to move that truck, buddy," the patrolman said. "You've got traffic stopped for two blocks."

The truck driver nodded toward Rennie. "Got a problem here, officer."

"I'm doing the best I can!" Rennie exploded. "I don't know why the thing won't start."

"Get down," the man in the suit ordered. It was a voice accustomed to being heeded.

"What?"

"Get down. Hand me the toolbox. It's under the seat there." He took off his suit jacket, looked around for a place to put it and then tossed it on the ground. One of the women onlookers picked it up and brushed it off. "Officer, if you could just guide those cars around the truck for a minute or two, I'll try to untangle this mess."

"I'll see what I can do, Mr. Blackstone," the policeman said.

Rennie looked at the man who was now climbing into the tractor seat. Her face flooded with color. It couldn't be Connor Blackstone! She held out the toolbox, swallowed and shrank back.

He tried starting the tractor, failed, then climbed down and leaned over the engine, studying the thing carefully.

"Ah, I see the problem," he said. "Fuel hose split. Right there where it joins the carburetor. Now, if there's enough slack in it, maybe I can just cut that piece off..." He worked at it briefly, reattached the hose and climbed back into the seat. After two coughing attempts the tractor sprang into life, and he neatly maneuvered it out of the delivery truck's way.

He got down and gave Rennie a withering look. "You have the wrong part on there. That's a vacuum hose, not a fuel hose."

"I...I didn't..." Rennie stammered. "I mean, it's not my tractor. I just borrowed it."

He didn't seem to be listening. He took out a handkerchief and wiped grease from his hands. Then he leaned down and wiped black dirt from his softly burnished shoes. Finally he stepped over to the newly placed trash can and with serious deliberation dropped the handkerchief into it. He turned, looked directly at Rennie, and for the first time his mouth turned up at the corners in a small quirky smile.

"Hope we don't run into this situation when that idiot parking garage goes up," he said. He thanked the woman who had been holding his coat and slipped it back on. A man in a dark suit and a chauffeur's hat had joined the onlookers.

"Okay, Frank, let's see how fast we can get through this mess," Blackstone said calmly, glancing at his watch and then striding across the street toward the waiting limousine.

"Thank you," Rennie murmured, knowing he couldn't possibly hear her above the din of traffic. She wondered how long it would take her to stop feeling like an absolute fool.

"Who was that?" Teddy asked.

"That was Mr. Blackstone. He owns this property."

The seven children absorbed the information thoughtfully.

"He sure knows all about tractors," Randolph said.

"IS MY FACE still red?" Rennie opened the kitchen door and let herself into the Kenyons' house, leaving Pete outside to run loose and explore.

"Oh, hi, Rennie." Sandy Kenyon glanced up from the cake she was icing with the aid of her sticky four-year-old. "There, Marcia, that'll do it. Wash your hands and go see if you can find daddy." She gave Rennie a quick perusal. "You're not talking about sunburn, I take it. What happened?"

Rennie sank into a chair across the table and breathed in the mingled odors of baking, something savory on the stove and honeysuckle wafting in through the screen.

"I had just a tiny bit of trouble with the tractor," she said. "I brought it back on the flatbed, by the way. It's right outside."

"What kind of trouble?" Sandy asked, looking concerned. Her sprinkling of freckles stood out, and her short auburn hair was curled tight against her head.

"Nothing serious. Fuel line split. It's all fixed."

"You fixed it?"

"No. Connor Blackstone fixed it, believe it or not."

Sandy stared at her. "You're kidding! Mr. Big himself?"

"He happened to be passing by. Oh, Sandy, I was mortified!" Rennie wailed. "He was all dressed up, going someplace in a big limo with a driver."

Sandy moved to the sink, urged Marcia to finish washing and herded her toward the back door. Then she returned to the table and began picking up bowls and spatulas.

"The thing is," Rennie explained in a rush, "I'd never met him because it was Mayor Wisner who spoke to him for us. Only yesterday, when we had a kind of a run-in about the trash they were throwing around, I sort of acted as if I had. I mean, I told him how Mr. Blackstone was so much in favor of this garden project and everything. Well, how was I to know? He was wearing work clothes and even a hard hat. He must have thought I was three kinds of a fool, and then seeing him again today...except today he was all dressed up in a suit. Oh, Sandy, I was so embarrassed!''

Sandy frowned and nodded. ''I'm sure that'll all make sense as soon as I have a chance to figure it out,'' she said cheerfully. ''Meanwhile, let's have something to eat. Here're the troops.''

The kitchen door banged open and Bob Kenyon came in, trailed by Marcia and six-year-old Jack, who gave Rennie a big gap-toothed grin.

Rennie repeated the story of the tractor mishap. Bob's forehead furrowed below his slightly receding hairline. ''Golly, I'm sorry about that, Rennie.''

''It wasn't serious,'' she insisted, ''and I want to pay you for a new fuel line. I'm sure there wasn't any damage done. I do appreciate so much your letting me borrow the tractor.''

''Just don't know how that happened.'' Bob shook his head and stroked his beard thoughtfully.

''Sounds like one of Bob's repair jobs.'' Sandy tossed her husband a grin. ''Probably grabbed the first thing he saw and stuck it on there.'' Bob Kenyon, college professor and part-time farmer, was not particularly known for his mechanical abilities.

''I might've at that,'' Bob agreed.

''Well—'' Rennie got to her feet ''—I've got to be getting home. Thanks again for everything you two have done. This whole project never would've gotten off the ground without you. And you don't even live in the school district!''

"Maybe that's why we wanted to do it," Bob said. "We feel pretty lucky out here. Those kids stuck in the city deserve a little help."

"Truly, Rennie, it's our pleasure. Now, don't even think about going home," Sandy said. "Stay for supper."

"Oh, no," Rennie protested. "You've both done so much already."

"Hey, don't think I've forgotten your promise to cook us a meal. But that can come later, when you've got this thing under way. Right now you'd better sit right there and dig in."

"I wouldn't argue with her," Bob warned in a whisper.

"Although it might not hurt to wash up first," Sandy suggested gently, flashing her husband a grin.

DARKNESS WAS NOT quite complete when Rennie arrived back in town, her spirits almost magically restored by the hour she'd spent in the Kenyons' happily untidy kitchen, eating chicken casserole, garden lettuce and lemon layer cake. Beside her Pete, also well fed, snoozed on the seat. Dusk was falling and the air had turned heavy and still. She drove her pickup down South Street toward the lot. It was a part of town that had been neglected in recent years. Once it had held trim houses and well-kept little yards, but that had been back in the prosperous days of the big Home Hearth Bakery. Now paint was peeling, buildings were abandoned, and people walked with their heads down, looking much like their houses, forgotten and defeated.

She pulled up beside the lot, parked and got out. Even with nothing planted yet, the plowed land improved the looks of the block. Rennie studied it in the twilight, mentally marking off the individual plots that would be allotted to the children and also to any adults from the neighborhood who showed an interest. That small shed in the far corner might serve as a place for tools and supplies, she thought, if it could be fitted with a stout padlock. Rennie had no illusions about everyone in the neighborhood being trustworthy. She drew a deep breath and reassured herself that fighting for the project *had* been the right thing. It *would* work, and even if it was only for one summer, perhaps next year another possibility would open up.

"Checking up on us again? I promise you, I've told all the men to be very neat."

Rennie gave a start and whirled around. Connor Blackstone stood there in the same gray suit from the afternoon, only now his collar and tie were loosened and his jacket unbuttoned. Both hands were thrust into his trouser pockets, and he was regarding her with interest. Or perhaps suspicion, she thought.

"Goodness, you scared me." His powerful masculine presence seemed to cast a force field around him. Rennie felt herself unaccountably drawn into it.

"I didn't think anything scared you, Miss..."

"Tate. Rennie Tate."

She could see his one-sided smile in the soft dusk. "Well, Miss Rennie Tate, you're putting in a long day, aren't you?"

"I really wasn't checking up on you," Rennie said in a rush. "I just wanted to look at the lot again, that's all. And I'm very sorry about this afternoon, Mr.... It is Mr. Blackstone, isn't it?"

"Connor."

"Well, I do apologize for all that business with the tractor. And for not recognizing you yesterday, too, when I, you know, when I yelled at you. I just didn't expect to find you on the job like that, and of course I'd never met you personally...even though I did sort of act as if I had." Once again she felt a flush of embarrassment. She noted that the impeccably tailored business suit did not conceal the powerful build beneath it.

"I take a personal interest in all my jobs," he said. "Once in a while I like to look in on things. And I was glad to be reminded how much I'm in favor of this project of yours," he added gravely.

Rennie looked away, out across the plowed earth. "I guess you really don't care for the idea."

"Oh, well, gardening's not exactly my thing," he said in an offhand way. "However, my father's into it, and he thinks it's a fine idea. He knows the mayor pretty well, so Dad did hold my feet to the fire, in a manner of speaking. Convinced me I could spare the lot for the summer."

Rennie was somehow disappointed that he'd been so remote from the decision. But what difference did it make? They had the use of the land, and it was the children who would benefit.

"So, are you satisfied with the way it's going?" he asked.

"It's wonderful," she breathed. "Even with nothing planted yet. I had to take a last look at it before I went home."

"I've been known to do that, too," he admitted, keeping his eyes on her.

"I've just come from returning the tractor," she said quickly, trying to cover up the confusion she felt in his presence. "My friends let me use it. Actually, everything's loaned or donated. We don't have any money." She caught her breath and added hastily, "Oh, not that I intend to ask you for anything. I mean, we're so grateful just to have the land for the summer."

His head tilted in a slight nod. Despite the failing light she could see him staring at her intently. Suddenly, not quite knowing why, she blurted out, "And it's not true what you said before—that nothing scares me. I'm scared quite a lot of the time."

"It doesn't show."

"Even so, I am. I mean, when I first got the idea for the garden I was really pumped up about it, driving my principal crazy, begging him to go to the school board with it."

"You're a teacher, then."

"Yes. Sixth grade. And then when it all worked out and we started yesterday, well, I was scared."

"Of what?" She was aware of a darkening that was more than just dusk. A storm must be moving in, she thought.

"Oh, I suppose of failing. Letting the kids down. They put such absolute trust in me, you know. And I kept thinking, what if nothing grows? Or what if—you know, this is a pretty tough neighborhood—what if somebody comes in and stomps on it? I mean, there's a whole lot of things that could happen."

"I'll have to let you in on Blackstone's first rule," he said gravely. "Never be afraid. And never worry about things you can't control."

Lightning streaked the distant sky, followed by a rumble of thunder. From the truck Pete let out a nervous whine. A sudden cool breeze made Rennie hug herself. What a smug bit of advice, she thought, suddenly irritated. The great Connor Blackstone was never afraid of anything—at least, that was the implication.

"I'd better be getting home," she said abruptly. "There's going to be a storm."

And as if in answer, another bolt of lightning, much closer, split the sky, followed quickly by a crash of thunder. Rennie gave a start and felt a pair of strong arms around her. For a heartbeat she allowed herself to react to the warmth, the strength, the sheer maleness of the man. Let herself feel, for that fleeting moment, protected, cared for. It wasn't a feeling she was used to, she thought wryly, and pulled away.

"Looks as if it's already here." His voice was level. He steered Rennie toward her pickup and helped her in, all in one smooth motion. *Something he does all the time,* she thought cynically. *Acts gallant and protective toward women. He's the type.* But she could feel his arms around her all the way home, and the storm breaking over her head was no more wild and frenzied than her emotions.

CHAPTER TWO

THE TELEPHONE was ringing next morning when Rennie and Pete got back from their early-morning run. They had covered only two miles, but Rennie decided she'd be exercising enough in the days and weeks to come. In fact, she could easily omit the run before breakfast, but it was a strong and established habit, as well as good for Pete.

She threw a towel around her neck and picked up the phone.

"Rennie, did I get you out of bed?" She recognized the familiar voice of Fred Swanson.

"Goodness no. Pete and I were out for a run. Just came in the door. What's up?"

"Well, head for the shower and get on over to the garden site. And don't say I never do you any favors. This is just a warning not to wear one of your usual outfits. We're having our pictures taken for the paper."

"Oh, Fred, no! Whose idea was that?"

"Haven't a clue. It was the mayor's secretary who called me. He's going to be there, too, of course. My wife made me phone you. Mona said you'd be mad enough to spit if you got there wearing your grubby clothes."

"Tell Mona thanks for me. Only I'm already mad enough to spit over the idea of any pictures at all."

"Oh, it could be worse," the principal said cheer-fully.

"Fred, you're too forgiving. You're going to be there, I hope."

"Yup, I've got my orders, too. See you later."

Pete was slurping loudly from his water dish as Rennie made for the shower. Only when the hot water began to hit her in sharp insistent needles did it occur to her whose idea this must have been. Big business-men seldom made philanthropic gestures in secret. No doubt Connor Blackstone figured on polishing up his public image by letting it be known that he'd donated land for the garden project. Her annoyance stepped up a notch, but mingled with it was an unsettling mem-ory of the two of them standing in the dusk the day before, the storm moving in on them, the air heavy with its coming. And then that clashing moment of lightning and thunder and his arms around her. It was an instinctive gesture, she told herself sensibly. Yet for that moment, she had to admit, she'd felt a wild re-sponse leap in her. And even more, she'd felt guarded, protected, cared for.

Rennie stopped in her soaping and scrubbing and let the water pour over her. In her whole life, had she ever felt that before? She searched back over the years. Never, she thought. No one had ever felt she needed looking after.

She turned off the water and stepped out of the shower, hurriedly toweling herself in the tiny bath-room.

Everything about her house was tiny, but she loved it and had never wanted more. Originally, it had been a carriage house at the end of a drive belonging to one of the fine old homes in the center of town. Now she rented it from Mrs. Bridgewater, and the rent was less than many would have paid because Mrs. Bridgewater liked having her there. As the elderly owner often remarked, "You can't beat having a tenant who knows how to restart your furnace's pilot light when it goes out." Rennie could have added, "Or install a new washer on a leaky faucet, patch a hole in ancient plaster, hang window shades." Still, she'd never minded, and she liked old Mrs. Bridgewater.

In addition to the bathroom and an equally compact kitchen, the little house had only one room, but it was light-filled and cheerful, a combination bedroom-living room. Rennie had hung colorful posters on the wall, built a bookcase to hide the bed, made patchwork pillows to brighten the couch and chairs. And even though she was used to it now, she never ceased to enjoy it. *My very own place,* she often thought. *My very own.*

Idly she wondered what sort of home Connor Blackstone lived in. A sleek condo in town if he was single, she supposed. An elegant country place with sloping lawns if he was married. She gave herself a shake. But of course he was married. Successful men, dynamic men always had wives and children.

She toweled her hair furiously and began to dress.

The rain the night before had left the streets looking clean and fresh, the city putting on its best face. Rennie had decided on beige slacks and a white cotton sweater with short sleeves. Nothing she normally would have dreamed of wearing for outdoor work, but she could return home later and change. Today she hoped to start measuring and marking out the garden plots with stakes and string, and there were donations of seeds and plants to be picked up at supply houses.

She was anxious to start planting quickly, before the children's enthusiasm lagged, and had already decided to plant radishes first, since they grew with such encouraging speed.

Fred Swanson was there ahead of her, his mahogany face shining with good humor. Fred's broad smile seldom deserted him. He was in what looked like a serious discussion with Teddy Pohl, first of the young contingent to arrive.

"What we have to do right off is make the land friable," Teddy explained. "That's what Miss Tate said. Friable means soft and easy to work. That's when we start planting."

Fred nodded seriously, absorbing this. Then, spotting Rennie, he called out, "I'm having a lesson in gardening."

"Well, you're going to need it when we assign you a plot. Where's everybody?"

He consulted his watch. "Ought to be here any minute. Rennie, this place looks great. You've really been working."

"It's coming along. Today I want to measure it off and give everybody an individual piece to work on."

"I hear you've met our benefactor."

"Connor Blackstone, you mean? Yes. How did you hear?"

The principal grinned. "A major traffic jam late in the afternoon doesn't go unnoticed around here."

Before Rennie could launch into an explanation, the mayor's car arrived. Then the photographer from the paper, an efficient-looking young woman in a khaki jumpsuit, pulled up, and an immediate conference started on how the picture should be arranged. The mayor suggested he might wield a shovel, and Rennie found herself torn between amusement and annoyance.

Sandy Kenyon pulled up in her old station wagon a moment later.

"Hi! Thought I'd find you here," she hollered through her open window. She got out and pulled a box from the rear. "Some extra tools I found lying around Bob's shed. Trowels and cultivators mostly. You know Bob—when he loses something he buys a new one and then after a while he finds the original. Hey, what's going on here?" She lowered her voice. "Isn't that the mayor? And why are you so dressed up?"

"Sandy, you're an angel. We can use all these things." Rennie drew her aside. "Somebody set up a publicity picture. Guess who," she added with a disparaging look.

"You mean Connor Blackstone?" Sandy whispered.

"Who else would think of it? Who has time for this?"

"A picture doesn't take long," Sandy said reasonably. She was giving Rennie a close look, and under her scrutiny Rennie found herself blushing. "Honestly, he doesn't sound that terrible to me."

"I didn't say he was terrible," Rennie said, but she was finding herself feeling awkward and tongue-tied. "Well, anyway, thanks for the tools, Sandy. You were sweet to think of it."

"Got to get to the feed store," Sandy said, adding mischievously, "Smile nice for the camera, dear."

Moments after she'd left, a blue Lexus swung over to the curb and Connor Blackstone got out. Rennie felt strength draining from her, leaving her weak-kneed and uncertain, and this annoyed her more than anything else about the situation. She tried to get control of her feelings, but she knew she was doing a bad job of it. Her mouth went dry. She fixed her face into what she hoped was an impassive expression. Blackstone scowled against the strong early sunlight, nodded perfunctorily to the mayor and then wheeled on her.

"Miss Tate, if you had to arrange something like this, I'd have appreciated a little advance notice." His voice was low and angry. "I have a meeting in the state capital in an hour, a helicopter's waiting for me at the airport, and my driver had to leave to attend his sister's wedding. I had to cancel a breakfast meeting with my board of directors, none of whom were happy about it. I'm thoroughly—"

"Wait a minute!" she interrupted, her control shattering as anger welled up inside her. "Don't lay this on *me*. I figured it was your idea. I didn't know a thing about it until Fred Swanson called me this morning, and I haven't had any breakfast myself, in case you're interested."

He stared at her for a moment, and she could tell he was mentally shifting gears.

"I see," he said coolly. "It must have been the mayor's idea then. Well, all right. Sorry." He paused, obviously reflecting on what she'd said. "You thought it was *my* idea?"

"I figured you might want a little publicity for all your public spiritedness," she said in an equally chilly voice.

"I don't care for publicity," he replied. "I only agreed to show up here this morning because I thought it might do some good to let people know about the changes taking place in the neighborhood. Now, do you think we could get this thing over with?''

"Some changes," Rennie muttered sarcastically, turning away. "Luxury condos."

He gave her a sharp look, but then had no chance to answer, for Fred Swanson moved forward to introduce himself and shake hands, after which the mayor, voluble and expansive, launched into an impromptu speech praising Blackstone's generosity. The garden project would be an important foundation stone in the city's renewal plans for the neighborhood, he insisted. Children began to arrive, and Rennie stepped aside to tell them about the picture.

In the end, it was the efficient young woman in the jumpsuit who pulled it all together, giving in to the mayor's authority only to the extent of allowing him to hold a shovel. Rennie, stiff and unsmiling, was posed on one side of him with the children crowded in front of her. Connor Blackstone stood on the mayor's other side, glowering, while Fred Swanson's cheerful smile beamed out over the mayor's balding head.

The moment the photographer had finished, Blackstone climbed back into his car and pulled away. Rennie watched him go, irritability mounting in her as she compared this morning's irascible mood with the gentler, almost sympathetic one of the night before. Then her attention was demanded by the young woman, who wanted the correct names to go under the picture. Rennie went over them with her, spelling carefully and making a deliberate effort to control the anger she was feeling. "Frederic Swanson—no *k* on the end. He's principal of East Side Elementary."

"Are the children all enrolled there? I'll put, 'And students from the school.'"

"I'd like each child's name mentioned," Rennie said firmly. "I'll spell them for you."

The young woman sighed and nodded.

Still, in spite of its unpromising beginning, the day proved to be one of accomplishment. Rennie made an effort to put aside the strange unsettled mood that Connor Blackstone seemed to instill in her each time they met. Garden plots were measured and marked off with stakes and each child assigned one. Paths were laid out so plantings would not be trampled. The first radish seeds were sown, and Teddy Pohl's Green Wonder bean was carefully planted, as well. A surprising number of other would-be gardeners of all ages presented themselves. Invariably the first question was, "Can anybody come here and plant stuff?"

"First come, first served," Rennie replied. "It's strictly a community project. Anybody from the neighborhood's welcome until we run out of space."

Several of the older men who'd been onlookers at the traffic jam now reappeared and said they'd like to join in. Their first remarks also ran to a pattern. "I used to have a garden when I was a boy." "Me and my wife kept a garden years ago."

"You're more than welcome," Rennie said to each of them. "You'll have to supply your own tools and things to plant. We've had some donations for the children, and if there's anything extra, plants or seeds, we'll share it."

When Randolph and Donald returned after lunch they brought with them an elderly woman in a housedress and a straw hat.

"This here's our grandma," Randolph explained. "She come to spend the summer with us. Can she work in the garden?"

The woman had bent down to touch the soil, testing it with her fingers. Rennie knew in an instant she'd probably gardened all her life.

"We'd be real glad to have you, Mrs...."

"Callie Burgess," the woman said, and the two shook hands. "Thought maybe I could give the boys some help."

"We can do better than that," Rennie said promptly. "You can have your own plot right next to theirs."

The woman's dark face glowed. "I sure would enjoy that."

Rennie had planned to go home and change before starting to work, but in the end she'd gotten so involved in the measuring and staking that she stayed as she was, reassuring herself that everything could be washed. By midafternoon she had assigned plots to everyone who had shown a genuine interest, including several more children and a few self-conscious teenagers. The empty lot was well on its way to being filled with enthusiastic gardeners of all ages, rank beginners as well as veterans.

When a truck pulled up bearing the logo Blackstone Landscaping, Rennie took a quick second glance and then watched curiously as a tall man with a thatch of white hair stepped down. A boy of about ten was with him. They stood for a moment looking around.

Rennie stepped forward. "Can I help you?"

The man said, "Would you be Miss Tate?"

"I am, yes."

"I'm Pat Blackstone, and this is my grandson, Scott."

Rennie looked from one to the other. The resemblance was unmistakable—clear blue eyes and ruddy complexion.

"You're Connor Blackstone's father, then?"

"I am. And this is his boy."

Something inside Rennie plummeted as the large suburban house, the slim stylish wife and handsome children took shape in her head again. But of course she'd known.

"How do you do," she said. "Mr. Blackstone—your son, that is—mentioned that you were very much in favor of this project. I want to thank you for supporting it."

He lifted a seamed hand, much grimed with dirt. "No thanks necessary. I like a garden—any garden, anywhere. It's my business. That's why I stopped by today. You're getting a late start on your planting, and seeds take some time to germinate, so I thought maybe you could use a few plants that are already started."

"We...we certainly could," she said haltingly. "The only thing is, there's been no money allotted for this project, and I'm afraid we couldn't—"

"Oh, no, nothing like that," he assured her hastily. "These are gifts. I want the children to have them."

Rennie was touched. "That's really very kind of you," she said. "I don't know how to thank you."

"No need for that," he said brusquely. "Scott and I'll hand 'em down to you. They ought to go in the ground right away. You have any access to water?"

"We haven't really arranged that yet," Rennie said, looking doubtful.

"No problem," he said breezily. "They've got water over there at the old bakery building. Outdoor spigot where they've been mixing concrete." He nodded toward the structure that was being transformed into condos. "Go ahead and help yourself."

Rennie glanced at him. "I guess not many people still remember when it was a bakery. I was pretty little when it closed."

"Well, I sure remember it. Best bread in town. Sad day when they shut down."

"Yes, it was."

While they talked, he was handing down flats and pots of healthy-looking plants. Tomatoes, squash, carrots. Even marigolds.

"Few of those planted in between helps keep the bugs off. Make it look nice, too," he said, and she nodded.

The boy was lining up the containers as his grandfather handed them to him. Once he stole a look at her, and Rennie smiled at him. There was no answering smile. Again she felt the rush of emotion as she saw Connor's features reflected in the young face.

"You come back and visit us again, won't you, Scott?" she said.

"Okay." He gave an indifferent shrug.

It was past six when Rennie arrived home, the beige slacks and white sweater considerably grimed. She tossed them into the hamper and trudged toward the shower, trying to relax and work out the day's tensions the way she usually did. Worked well for tired muscles, but was less successful for her thoughts, which had coiled themselves into an impossible tangle. What had happened to her ability to cope with the most difficult situations? How could it be that all at

once she was at the mercy of an unwanted emotion?
And what was that emotion, anyway? Not attraction,
certainly. Absolutely not. The last thing she wanted
was entanglement with a man so clearly accustomed to
having his own way. And besides, she knew now that
he was married, and that put him beyond reach, even
if she felt the tiniest attraction for him. Which she did
not. Rennie wrenched the faucets off and reached for
a towel, trying to shut her thoughts off as well, only to
realize that someone was knocking on her front door.

With an exclamation of annoyance she grabbed her
white terry robe from its hook and wound a towel
around her wet hair. Mrs. Bridgewater had a habit of
appearing on her doorstep, sometimes to announce a
leaky radiator, sometimes to present her with half a
cake, saying, "Much too large for me, dear. You finish it."

Barefoot, she hurried to fling open the door.

Connor Blackstone stood there, a quizzical smile on
his face. He was casually dressed in a soft blue knit
shirt and chinos, and he was leaning with one hand
against the door frame as if he'd been there for some
time.

"I was sure you must be home—I saw your truck
parked in the drive." His gaze traveled over her, taking in the towel-wrapped hair, the bare feet, the white
robe cinched at her slender waist and the deep V in
front, which she now clutched nervously with one
hand.

Rennie, dumbfounded, stared back at him. Bursting in without any notice was probably typical of a
man who was so used to calling all the shots he simply
never thought about another person's convenience.
But why wasn't he headed out to the suburbs to that

elegant house with the sloping lawns, that sleek wife and those children who looked like him?

"I felt I had to apologize," he said. "I was unreasonable this morning. Very bad tempered. If I'd stopped to think for even a minute, I'd have recognized Mayor Wisner's fine hand in all those arrangements. Am I forgiven?"

"It's not important," Rennie said as coolly as she could, considering she was dripping water on the floor. And of course it wasn't important, not really, but other things were. "I met your father this afternoon." She paused. "And your son."

Something that looked like uneasiness crossed his rugged features. He glanced down at the wet footprints on the floor. "I wonder if I might come inside for a minute."

Rennie hesitated. "Was there something . . . ?" She let the question trail off.

"Just for a minute," he repeated, and at last she stepped back, letting him in.

She was ill at ease, but felt once again the power of his personality, which seemed to fill the little house like a gust of fresh wind.

"I've interrupted you," he said. "Please. Go ahead. I'll wait."

She was about to make a sharp reply, then reconsidered. She was not exactly at her best with her head in a towel and a damp robe clinging to her.

"I won't be a minute," she said, keeping her voice level.

She slipped back into the bathroom, dressed herself hastily in jeans and sandals and a clean white shirt. She did the best she could at combing her short wet hair and in moments was back in the main room. He was standing in the middle of her big braided rug, looking around.

"What an attractive house you have," he murmured. His scrutinizing gaze swung around to her. Rennie felt it like an unexpected wave of heat. She kept a tight grip on her composure, determined this time not to be swept along by his strong presence.

"Thank you." She waited, arms folded in front of her. Whatever he'd come here for, she was not going to make it easy for him.

He swung his gaze back to her and, as if in imitation of her, folded his arms across his chest.

"You said something this morning. I didn't have a chance to follow up on it, but I definitely heard it. You said 'luxury condos.'"

"What about it?"

One eyebrow lifted in a quizzical expression. "It was the way you said it. I got the feeling you disapprove of my plans to upgrade South Street."

"It's not my business," Rennie said.

He paused briefly, then, "I live in a remodeled town house on Berkeley Street. You know the ones? I bought the entire block and had them all renovated. It was a neighborhood that had been going downhill for years. Is there something wrong with attractive housing, in your view?"

She was almost distracted from what he was saying by the revelation he'd made. Suburban vistas vanished as she saw him now with his family in the elegant town house on Berkeley Street, a street she knew well. He seemed to be waiting for her answer.

"No, of course not," she said. "But what might be right for Berkeley Street could be altogether wrong for South Street."

"Is that what you think?"

"Yes, I do."

Both eyebrows went up this time. "Well, it's refreshing to meet someone who isn't reluctant to speak her mind."

She gave him a cynical look. "Oh, come now, Mr. Blackstone. We both know you don't think that. I suspect you don't like anybody disagreeing with you."

He unfolded his arms and put his hands on his hips in a casual, almost lazy stance. "How did I get on the wrong side of you so fast, Miss Tate?"

"You don't have to call me Miss Tate," she said irritably.

"Fine. Rennie, then. But you must call me Connor. And what's the answer to my question?"

She shrugged and walked to the window, where a purple clematis, climbing the outside wall, was pushing into view.

"I have a way of blurting things out," she admitted. "It's gotten me into trouble sometimes. Just forget it."

He followed her and stood beside her at the window. In spite of herself, Rennie glanced up at him. He was looking at her so intently she had to turn away. She tried to hang on to her poise.

"What is it that you disapprove of so much?" he persisted.

For several heartbeats there was silence between them. Then Rennie said, "I grew up in that South Street neighborhood. I was just like the kids you saw there this morning. I know the area well, and I hate seeing it turned into... what you're making it."

He spread his hands, palms up. "What am I doing that's so terrible?"

She sighed. "Nothing, the way you see it. But those luxury condos of yours aren't going to help the people who live there."

He said coldly, "I'm not a social worker."

Her mouth twisted in a small bitter smile. "You see? We really have nothing to say to each other. Time to head home to your wife and family, Mr. Blackstone." She started to walk away from him, but his hand shot out to grab her arm. His touch made her nerve endings tingle maddeningly.

"Wait a minute. What are we really talking about here? Is it just that you don't approve of me in general?"

"As a matter of fact, I don't," she said in a crisp tone. "But that has nothing to do with...anything else. I'm still very grateful that you lent us the land for the garden. I want you to know I appreciate that very much. We all do."

He stared down at her with a look so piercing she felt he was probing the twisted jumble of her thoughts, seeing the telltale hot responses her body was sending out in spite of herself. Then without warning he bent and took her in his arms, pulling her so tight to him that she could feel the muscular strength of his body, the length of his long sinewy frame. His mouth sought hers in a sudden powerful kiss. Rennie went limp in his arms, leaning into the kiss, into his arms, unable to stop herself.

For a moment the two of them stood by the window in a suspension of time. Then slowly, gently, he released her.

"You're welcome," he whispered. And before she could find enough breath to answer, he strode to the door. He turned then, looking back at her with a smile that was almost insolent. "And I'm not married," he said.

CHAPTER THREE

DURING THE NEXT FEW DAYS, work at the garden took on a repetitive routine that Rennie found reassuring, particularly since she didn't see or hear from Connor Blackstone again. But why should she? A casual kiss certainly wasn't any sort of commitment. And even though it might seem to her that "casual" was hardly the right word for the bone-shaking reaction she'd had to the touch of his lips on hers, it was obvious that's what it had been for him. Still, she found herself glancing too often across the lot in the direction of the old bakery, and if she was disappointed that he never appeared again, she managed to keep the feeling pushed down deep where it didn't show. There was plenty to do each day. Later, she told herself, when the garden was well established, she would try to think of some other activities to keep the kids busy. And herself, as well, she added.

Once plants and seeds were in the ground, there was time to work on the paths and borders. Pat Blackstone appeared one day with a length of wire fencing he swore he had no use for, although Rennie didn't really believe him. He helped her install it along the street side of the garden to set it off attractively and to keep out unthinking trespassers who might step on seedlings.

"That's perfect, Mr. Blackstone!" Rennie exclaimed as they stood back to admire it. "I can't thank you enough for all you've done."

"It's not work to me," the white-haired man said. "Any time I'm doing something in a garden, it's recreation."

"You certainly picked the right business, then."

"I suppose I did. Never thought of doing anything else."

"You haven't brought your grandson back," Rennie said tentatively.

He tossed a shovel into his truck. "No, he's off at some day camp. What's it called now?" He frowned, trying to remember. "Camp Windswept, I think."

"Oh, I see." Rennie had heard of Camp Windswept. It was no ordinary camp with basket weaving and marshmallow roasts, but an exclusive place near the shore with horseback riding, sailboarding, tennis, sailing, even polo—all for children whose parents were able to afford its hefty fees. She asked no more questions, not wanting to appear curious, even though the subject of Connor Blackstone and his son kept bouncing around her mind in an infuriating way. *I'm not married,* he'd said, so of course she'd deduced that there had been a divorce. More than likely his son was spending the summer vacation with him. And what business was it of hers, anyway?

Now every day the garden was busy with workers, both children and adults, and the first tender plants were appearing, putting down roots and taking hold in the newly tilled and enriched soil.

Callie Burgess showed up each day with her grandsons, Randolph and Donald, and her knowledge seemed endless. "When those get started a little more, you want to pinch 'em back to make 'em stronger.'' Or, "Now dig a little bitty well around that plant and bank it up in the middle. Don't handle it rough, child. It's just a baby."

Only a few plots remained to be spoken for, and Rennie had no doubt they'd all be taken before long. The story and picture in the daily paper had brought out several more gardeners and some contributions from local businesses, including more plants and three bales of peat moss.

Then one day Rennie happened to glance over toward the old bakery building, and her heart gave a bouncing leap as she recognized Connor Blackstone's tall broad-shouldered form. He was talking with one of the workers, who Rennie now knew was the foreman. She looked away quickly and concentrated hard on the zinnia seeds she was sowing along the newly installed fence.

When a shadow fell across her a few minutes later, her hands grew still, but she didn't look up. A familiar voice said, "You seem to be making very good progress."

Rennie tilted her head up at last and then rose slowly. He was dressed for business again today, and somehow in the expensively tailored suit he was less approachable, not at all same man who had stood in her little house, looking around quizzically. And certainly not the same man who had pulled her against him in that swift impulsive kiss.

"I think we're doing quite well," she murmured.

He was studying her, and she could tell there was more he wanted to say.

"I've been out of town for a few days," he said. "My father's given me reports, though."

"He's been so helpful. This fence was his idea." She waited a moment and then, as the silence grew awkward, she said, "I was just putting in some zinnia seeds . . ."

At the same time he said, "There was something I wanted to ask . . ."

They both laughed and Rennie said, "You wanted to ask me something?" She wished she could be more natural around him, but her mouth had gone dry and her hands were trembling.

"Yes. Actually, a kind of favor." He paused and seemed to be choosing his words carefully. He might be seeking a favor, but there was nothing indecisive about his attitude, Rennie thought. It was probably the way he was in the boardroom when making rulings about the disposition of hundreds of thousands of dollars—crisp and authoritative. She waited for him to go on.

"It's about Scott," he said finally.

"Your son."

"Yes. It occurred to me he might get a lot out of coming here to work in the garden with the other kids." He spoke in a brisk positive way. This was obviously something he'd worked out in his mind, and having decided on it, he wanted to implement it as speedily and efficiently as possible.

Rennie could only stare at him for a moment as she thought of a rich man's son moving from the rarefied atmosphere of Camp Windswept to this run-down part of town. Without meaning to, she glanced at red-headed Becky, toiling and sweating over some new tomato plants, at Teddy Pohl kneeling in the dirt, earnestly watering what he'd just set out, and at Callie Burgess in her housedress and ragged straw hat.

Rennie stalled, trying to think of the right answer. "Uh, your father told me he was spending the summer at camp."

Connor made an impatient gesture with one hand. "That wasn't such a great idea, I'm afraid. I don't think he's getting much out of it."

Rennie, accustomed to the ways of ten-year-olds, could translate that answer easily. The kid had put his foot down, declared he wouldn't go back to that crummy place, maybe even had a temper tantrum. Still, this lot belonged to Blackstone; she couldn't possibly be ungracious about his request.

"Of course he's more than welcome to join us," she said, hoping she didn't sound reluctant. "Only...have you asked him about it? Does he want to?"

His mouth clamped into a line. "I'm not sure he knows what he wants," he admitted woodenly. "It seems to me it would be good for him."

Rennie refrained from saying she had serious reservations about that. "Well, then, by all means, bring him along," she said, keeping her voice light. "Of course you understand this isn't exactly like a playground program. I mean, the kids are free to come and go. I'm just around to keep an eye on the garden and answer questions, help them out. It's really a community enterprise."

"Yes, but you're here most of the time, aren't you?" he persisted.

"Well, I have been, but that's because we're just getting it started. I can't actually promise—"

"I'm not worried about that," he interrupted briskly as if he'd considered it and come to a decision. "I'm sure it'll work out all right. I think it will do Scott a lot of good."

Rennie felt her heart sinking. That was twice he'd mentioned that it would be good for Scott. His son's welfare was obviously uppermost in his mind. And equally obvious was the fact that he was pleased to have found someone he trusted to take care of Scott. A capable baby-sitter, Rennie thought as disappointment welled up inside her.

Connor gave her a long look, and Rennie, interested in spite of herself, gazed back at him. His mouth, strong yet sensual, was for the moment softened. Rennie remembered with a powerful jolt what those lips had felt like pressed against hers.

"Rennie..." He paused, and the summer day was suddenly quiet around them, all sounds coming as if from a distance. The moment stretched out. Then, returning to himself, Connor became businesslike. "Fine, then," he said. "I'll drop him off tomorrow." He strode away without another word, and Rennie, her trowel clutched in one hand, watched him go.

Slowly she knelt and worked the soil. Bitterness, an unfamiliar feeling with her, began to rise slowly, all the way from her toes to her hairline.

Of course, she thought. He was a businessman, and a consummate one. This was what he did. It was what he was good at. He manipulated people, and before they knew what was happening, they were doing what he wanted. He'd spotted her from the first as someone who might be useful to him. He'd seen her with the children and he knew she was a teacher. His father, probably unwittingly, had reinforced the idea. When he'd come to her house he'd said it was to apologize for his behavior, but soon enough he'd advanced from that to the real ingratiating process, starting off by telling her how much he liked her home.

And wasn't that a hoot—someone who lived in an elegant town house on Berkeley Street admiring that little shoebox of hers. Rennie pressed her lips together tightly to keep them from trembling. After that he'd brought out the heavy artillery and kissed her. Then, when he had her pliant and responsive he'd left, playing it cool for the next few days so that she'd be wondering if she was ever going to see him again.

Her bitterness turned to blood-rushing anger as Rennie blindly jammed seeds into the ground. He was a manipulator, that was what he was. Taking what he wanted from this neighborhood without a thought about the people who lived in it, taking advantage of *her* because he'd known she'd never turn down a child in need. And if the boy proved difficult, why, he'd have deftly passed that problem on to someone else, wouldn't he? To her dismay she felt her eyes fill with tears.

"Ain't you sowing them seeds a little deep, Rennie?" Callie sounded concerned. "Don't hardly believe the sun's gonna reach 'em a foot underground."

For the first time, Rennie realized that she'd been stabbing the seeds into the soft dirt with furious energy.

"Oh, Callie." She sat back on her heels. "I wasn't thinking. What's the matter with me?"

The old woman replied gently, "Here, lemme give you a hand with that." She knelt beside Rennie and took the packet from her, pouring the seeds into one worn palm and then distributing them along the fence and covering them lightly with soil. She kept her eyes on her work while Rennie made two smudgy swipes at her teary eyes.

The next morning, when Connor Blackstone delivered his son to the garden, along with a few more flats of young plants sent by Pat, Rennie was better prepared for him. She smiled a determined smile at both father and son, then turned all her attention to the boy, scarcely noticing when Connor left.

"Did you ever have a garden of your own, Scott?" she asked.

The boy kept his eyes averted, slightly off to one side. "Nope."

"Your granddad being in the business, I thought you might have."

"I help Grandpa sometimes, that's all."

"Is it fun?"

He shrugged. "It's okay, I guess."

The other kids, now numbering about a dozen, stared curiously at the new arrival. With Pete trotting behind them, Rennie led Scott along the paths until they reached a staked-off plot that had not yet been claimed. It adjoined Becky Harmon's. Becky, who was never late, was already on her hands and knees, pulling up a few small weeds.

"Becky, this is Scott," Rennie said. "I'm letting him have the plot next to yours. Maybe you can give him some pointers on getting started."

"Okay," Becky said, showing no great enthusiasm. Then she added with some importance, "I'm mulching today."

"Big deal," Scott said under his breath.

Rennie decided to overlook that and said cheerfully, "The ground's been turned over, but you'll want to work on it a little more to get it nice and soft. Here's a cultivator you can use."

"I brought my own," the boy said. "My grandpa gave it to me. I brought my own plants, too. Tomatoes and zucchini and carrots and beets. I can have all I want."

Rennie was uncomfortably aware of all the eyes trained on them. "Well, fine," she said. "Better get at it, then. There are watering cans back there by the shed. We're allowed to get water from next door where the men are working."

"Yeah, I know. That's my dad's place."

"Then I guess you can get started." Rennie's good cheer was wearing desperately thin, but she knew that the most irritating children were generally the ones most in need of love. "I'll be around later to see how you're doing."

As she started away he asked suddenly, "Is that your dog?"

She turned back. "Yes. His name's Pete."

When Scott looked away without responding, she headed back to the fence.

A man was standing on the path beside her freshly planted zinnias. Memory stirred inside her.

"Mr. Steele?" she said, surprised.

He smiled and nodded. "Little Rennie Tate. Saw your picture in the paper." They shook hands warmly.

"I'd have known you anywhere!" Rennie exclaimed, although she had to admit he'd changed. He was older, his hair thinner and grayer, his shoulders stooped. "All those Saturday mornings I used to come to the bakery for fresh bread, and you used to ask me when I was going to get up really early and surprise you. But of course I never could."

"No, because I got up at four to get the dough mixed and the ovens heated up."

"Well, you certainly made the best bread in town. And isn't it funny—I was just talking to somebody about that." Rennie thought of Pat Blackstone, who'd said the same thing.

"I miss the old place," the man said, as his welcoming grin faded. "Looks like it's getting fancied up some."

"They're making condos out of it."

"Do tell. And we're eating bread from some out-of-town bakery."

"I'm afraid so."

He shook his head as if trying to figure it out. "Well, no matter. Actually I came by to see if you've got a corner of this garden left for me."

"You mean you want to garden with us? Oh, Mr. Steele, I'm so pleased. Will your wife be coming, too? I remember her well from when she used to help out at the bakery."

A cloud passed over his features. "No, my wife passed away five years back."

"Oh, I'm so sorry."

"Well, those things happen," he said, with a small helpless gesture of one hand. "It was a long illness and hard on her. After she was gone I sold the house—good many bills to pay, you know. I moved in with my sister and rented a room from her. Only I don't have a garden anymore." Rennie recalled the Steeles' little house, the tiny front garden bursting with flowers and vegetables every summer.

She said quickly, "And you must miss it. Oh, I'm so glad you came before all the spaces were taken. Come on, I'll show you a nice plot, back in the corner by the shed. I was sort of saving it for someone special."

As they walked to the plot, Rennie told him where she lived now.

"Oh, sure, I know where that is. Used to be the old McAndrew property." He nodded. "And you're a schoolteacher, just like your mom and dad. Where are they now?"

"Out on the West Coast. And still teaching."

"Do tell." He shook his head again.

"Here we are." Rennie stopped and waved a hand at the empty corner of the lot. The weathered-looking shed stood against the property line with a row of spindly little trees behind it, half hiding the back of the garage next door and a few junked cars.

"Your plot would run from the edge on those two sides," Rennie explained, pointing. "And the shed would be included in it. That part's a little shaded in the afternoon. But the rest of it, over on this side, gets lots of sunshine the whole day. It's larger than some of the ones the children have, but you might enjoy working on it."

She saw his eyes moving around and knew that in his mind it was already planted and flourishing.

"Looks like a real nice spot to me," he said happily. "I sure appreciate it."

Rennie smiled at him. "We're getting a rather late start. I just couldn't manage to get everything arranged earlier."

"Then all the more reason not to waste time," he said, clapping his hands with enthusiasm. "I'll fetch my tools and be right back."

Rennie waved him off, noticing that his step was already lighter and more energetic.

As she turned back, a flurry of angry voices erupted. Rennie glanced around to see where it was

coming from and saw a scuffle in progress between
Becky and Scott. Pushing was being replaced by hit-
ting, and as Rennie dashed toward them she saw the
sturdy Becky bring a sweeping fist around to catch the
boy just in front of his left ear. He howled and shoved
her into the dirt.

"Becky! Scott! Stop that this minute!" she shouted.
"What's going on?" She pulled Becky to her feet and
dusted her off, holding her firmly to keep her from
swinging again. Scott stood glowering at the girl.

"I'm ashamed of both of you," Rennie scolded.
"Who started all this?"

"He yanked out one of my tomato plants!" Becky
stormed.

"It was on my side. You planted it in the wrong
place!"

Rennie could see a raised welt on his head where
Becky's fist had connected. What would Connor
Blackstone say when he saw his son? She felt her heart
sink with dread.

Rennie frowned severely at both of them. "Rule one
in this garden," she said to Scott. "We never damage
a healthy plant no matter where it's growing. And rule
two, Becky, we never start fights with anyone. Under-
stood?"

"It was on my side of the string," Scott insisted
sullenly.

"It was not! Maybe it was on the line, that's all."

"All right, if it was on the line, couldn't you have
shared the tomatoes when they appeared?" Rennie
asked. "Now neither of you will have them."

"I want a different plot," Scott said, kicking up a
clod of dirt.

"Great idea!" Becky exploded. "Give him one far away from me."

"This is the one you were assigned, Scott," Rennie said. "I see no reason to give you another. And if either of you creates a scene like this again, you won't be allowed to come to the garden anymore."

Becky's lower lip shot out belligerently as she held back tears, and Rennie had to resist the temptation to give her a reassuring hug. Scott aimed another kick into the dirt, left his trowel, cultivator and plants lying there and stomped off. Rennie followed him as he headed for the building next door.

At the edge of the garden he paused, stiff and furious. Rennie caught up with him.

"Would you like me to phone your father or your grandpa to come and pick you up?" she asked softly. "You don't have to stay, you know."

"You don't want me to stay, anyway," he said, his small features pinched with anger.

"Of course I want you to stay. But I can't make you."

Pete, who had followed, sat between them looking with concern at first one then the other. Suddenly he got up, stood on his short hind legs and put both front feet on Scott's thigh. The boy looked down at him, surprise crowding the fury out of his face.

"There now," Rennie said. "You've just made your first friend."

Scott reached down and patted Pete's head with a small grubby hand. Rennie stayed quiet for a moment, letting him collect himself, then suggested, "While we're over here, let's get some cold water for that bump on your head."

But the boy shook her attentions off. "I don't need any water," he said. "It's no big deal."

Connor Blackstone, when he arrived to pick up his son late that afternoon, took a different view.

"What happened to him?" he demanded of Rennie when he caught sight of Scott.

Rennie drew a deep breath. She was looking, too. The boy was covered with dirt, flushed and sweating. The lump in front of his ear was still red and sore-looking. He and Becky had worked side by side through most of the afternoon without speaking to each other, but the strain was beginning to show. Staying silent was too much for them. Slowly they'd begun to exchange a few scattered resentful words, and Randolph had come over to examine their progress and offer suggestions. Pete completed the circle.

"Gardening's a fairly dirty business, you know," Rennie said.

"I'm not talking about dirt. What's that swelling on his head?" He scowled down at her. "Did he fall?"

She sighed. "No, he didn't fall. Someone took a swing at him."

"What?" His face flushed angrily. "Is that the best you can do to keep these kids in line? Look, it's not that I want somebody to fight my kid's battles for him, but it seems to me the least you could do is to keep an eye on the ones who act aggressive. What'd he do, anyway, to deserve that?"

Rennie kept her voice calm, ignoring the rush of adrenaline that surged every time she stood close to him. "He pulled up one of Becky's tomato plants."

"Becky's..." He looked back at the three children. "A girl did that?"

"Becky's a fairly strong girl."

His expression was so uncertain that Rennie wanted at first to laugh and then longed to put out a hand to him, to reassure him by her touch that it really would be all right. As he started for the boy she said quickly, "Connor—" and then stopped, because it was the first time she'd spoken his name, and she thought it must sound as strange to him as to her.

He turned to her.

"Don't mention the lump to him."

His face darkened. "Thank you." His voice was frosty. "I appreciate your interest, but I think I know how to treat my own son." With a last angry glare, he strode toward Scott.

When they'd left, Rennie stood where she was for a long time, wondering why life had such an irritating way of holding out something wonderful and then abruptly snatching it back. *And you didn't do a bad job yourself, Rennie Tate,* she said silently. If she'd wanted to alienate Connor Blackstone, she couldn't have picked a surer way than implying he wasn't a good father.

CHAPTER FOUR

RENNIE WAS SURPRISED when the blue Lexus pulled up the next morning and Scott climbed out. The car left at once, before she even had a glimpse of Connor, but she was almost relieved. It was hard enough to act normally around him when things were going well. His resentment the day before indicated that he expected some Olympian judgments from her when a difficult situation arose. But what was so difficult, really, about two kids having a little dustup? It happened all the time on the playground, and what you did was ignore it and go on as before. Of course, to be quite honest, that's what Connor had done, hadn't he? Bringing the boy back this morning seemed to indicate he wanted everything to carry on normally. Rennie's thoughts twisted this way and that as she tried to understand a man who seemed remote and unapproachable one moment and appealing and vulnerable the next.

"Hello, Scott." She smiled widely at the boy as he approached. She could see that the swelling had gone down, although the spot was now turning several interesting colors.

He didn't return her smile. "Hi," he said. He paused long enough to lean over and stroke Pete's head, then moved off toward his garden plot. Becky, who was already at work with a watering can, gave him a cool glance.

"Hi," he said.

"Hi." Becky went on with her watering, but Rennie, turning away, smiled to herself. The fight was already history. It occurred to her that adults could take a lesson from kids when it came to matters of holding grudges.

Mr. Steele had arrived earlier and was hard at work in his corner near the shed. He'd brought tools and plants in a wheelbarrow and was busy digging up neat rows and yanking some weeds close to the shed. Teddy Pohl and Randolph had their heads together as they studied seed packets, and six-year-old Donald, with his shorter attention span, was squatting near his grandmother making mud pies. One by one others began to arrive, and soon the whole place was busy with quiet activity. The only sounds were the children's voices, the scratching of a hoe or now and then a burst of laughter on the morning air. Rennie thought back to what the vacant lot had looked like that first day—littered with trash, overrun with weeds and as hard as stone, a sorry desolate place. She allowed herself some wishful thinking. If only more people gardened... If only there were more green spaces among the concrete and glass blocks of cities... If only—

"No, Pete!" The young voice was commanding, and Rennie whirled to see where it had come from. Scott Blackstone had a firm grip on Pete's collar and one finger of his other hand was raised in admonishment.

Rennie started to speak, then saw what the trouble was. The same thin half-wild cat that had caused such a crisis a week ago had crept up close to where Scott and Becky were working. Pete was trembling from nose to tail and eyeing the intruder with fierce concentration, but Scott restrained him. And restrained him effectively, Rennie saw with astonishment. She doubted whether she could have done as well. She could almost see in the child the forceful decisiveness so apparent in his father, the natural air of command.

She grabbed Pete's leash and hurried over, but instead of snapping it on his collar, she handed it to Scott and let him do it.

"You can put him in the truck," Rennie said, and Scott did so, once more shaking a finger at Pete and addressing him firmly.

Rennie doubted that Pete would stay in the truck with a cat on the loose. But miraculously he did. He rested his chin on the open window and shook with excitement, but he stayed.

By the time Scott returned, several heads had turned to observe the situation, and Randolph strolled over for a better look at the feline intruder, who was crouching at a safe distance.

"Ain't much of a cat, is it?" Randolph said, appraising it.

"No, but it's probably hungry," Scott said.

Rennie watched the two boys approach the animal slowly, but as soon as they got near, it retreated. She saw their two heads come closer together as they conferred, their voices low. Presently they approached her.

"Miss Tate," Scott said, "me and Randolph think we'd better get some food for that cat."

Rennie hesitated. "He certainly looks as if he could use it," she admitted.

"There's a grocery store just down the street there," Randolph said with a wave of his hand.

"Well . . . all right. But you'll need some money."

"I've got money," Scott said.

Should she allow it? Rennie examined the problem quickly. Presumably his father had given him spending money, but for ice cream or a cold drink, not for cat food. Still, what harm could it do?

"Okay," she agreed after a moment. "Better get the dry food that comes in a box. It goes further."

"I'll see what they have." Scott's face was serious as he considered it.

Rennie watched the two boys hurry off, the odd notion rattling around in her head that she'd just seen Connor as a small boy. That's exactly the way he must have been. Serious about approaching a problem, but decisive, not hesitating once he saw what had to be done. Thinking about him started a confused reaction in her, a rush of warmth quickly blocked by the remembrance of his chilliness the day before. It might be better, she advised herself severely, to stop being sentimental and confusing the boy with the man. Scott was an unusual kid, true enough, but he was just himself, a lively ten-year-old. Connor Blackstone was another matter entirely.

Interest in the cat provided a diversion for the remainder of the day. When Scott and Randolph returned with a box of food, an immediate search was started for a dish. Mr. Steele provided it—the plastic top of a coffee can in which he'd brought powdered plant food.

"Might be thirsty, too," Callie Burgess called out.

The boys ran next door to the renovation site, and one of the workmen trimmed a soft-drink cup with his pocket knife to a size a cat could reach. They filled it at the outdoor faucet and hurried back.

Despite a full dish of food and fresh water, the circle of staring faces made the cat retreat in terror behind the spindly trees near the shed.

"Why don't we leave him be?" Mr. Steele suggested. "Go about our business and don't pay him any mind. Then I'll bet he'll come out and eat."

It was difficult to persuade Donald, who kept calling, "Kitty, kitty," and chasing the frightened animal, but Callie succeeded in coaxing him away with the promise of a story. Donald subsided immediately and sat down to listen, and the cat was for a time forgotten.

"Miss Tate."

Rennie looked up in surprise. Scott had come up to her quietly.

"Look, Miss Tate."

Rennie followed his glance. The stray cat had crept out from the shelter of the saplings and was crouching over the makeshift food dish, eating hungrily. Rennie looked at Scott and saw that for the first time he was grinning at her.

"Good job, Scott," she said.

Randolph joined them, and the three of them watched for several minutes. Suddenly Rennie frowned, looked closer and sighed. "Oh, dear."

Both boys turned to her, questions on their faces.

"That cat's not a he, boys, it's a she." She turned and called softly, "Callie, have you taken a good look at that cat?"

The old woman bobbed her head and then turned to smile at Rennie from under her hat. "Wondered how long it was gonna take you to notice."

"Oh, dear," Rennie repeated with a shake of her head.

"Yup. The poor thing's probably gonna have kittens," Callie said.

"Hey, that'd be great!" Randolph exclaimed.

The gardeners drifted off around lunchtime, but most of them returned. The younger children were now enchanted with the idea of the cat, and the older ones seemed to be finding the place a good spot for getting together. But before long, the teenagers headed for the municipal pool. The others spent the late afternoon watching Mr. Steele organize his garden. As he worked, he explained what he was doing, and then, when he'd done enough plowing for one day, as he put it, he opened a big bag and brought out cookies for everyone. For Rennie he'd brought a loaf of bread he'd baked that morning.

"Can't get over those early-rising habits," he said.

Rennie told the children that Mr. Steele had been a baker years before and that she had gone to that very building—she pointed to it—to buy bread from him. "When I was almost your age," she said, and they all stared at her in wonder and some disbelief.

Then at last it was time to leave. Scott and Randolph refilled the cat's dish and brought fresh water, and one by one the gardeners drifted home until only Rennie and Scott were left.

Rennie expected each car that went by to be the blue Lexus, or at least the pickup belonging to Scott's grandfather, but neither one appeared. Rennie peeked at her watch.

"Who was supposed to come for you, Scott?" she asked finally.

The boy frowned. "I don't know for sure. But I know the way to Dad's house. I can walk."

Rennie was touched that he said, "Dad's house," rather than "our house." Evidently it was still not entirely home to him.

"Oh, I don't think that's such a good idea," she said. "If there's been a mix-up, you might find no one there. Apparently signals got crossed somewhere. Tell you what—you come home with me." It was most unlikely that Connor Blackstone's house would be empty. There'd certainly be a maid or housekeeper there, Rennie thought, yet she sensed that the little boy was often lonely, and she'd seen his eyes brighten at her suggestion.

"You bring Pete," she said. "I'm sure no one will worry. They'll know you're with me."

"Okay," he agreed. Pete, who'd been let out on a leash after the first excitement over the cat had subsided, was helped back into the pickup, and Scott climbed in after him. "He's got himself pretty dirty," he observed, one arm around the dog as they started out. "I think he's been rolling in something."

"I think so, too," Rennie agreed. "He's also taken to visiting the workmen next door. Some of that's probably concrete dust. Why don't you give him a bath when we get home?"

The boy's head turned to her quickly. "No kidding?"

Rennie swung the pickup in a left turn. "He sure needs it."

Scott was in the middle of the operation, only slightly less soapy than Pete, when the blue Lexus pulled into her long driveway an hour later. Rennie had changed into denim shorts, an oversize T-shirt and sandals and was working in her tiny kitchen, looking out at the bathing now and then. When she saw the car, her heart did a sudden leap, then began to beat furiously. This might not have been one of her better ideas, she thought in a panic. What would she say to him? They'd parted stiffly the day before, and he'd as much as accused her of being lax in her supervision of the children. She stopped slicing mushrooms, dried her hands on a towel and went outside.

She knew the moment she saw his face that he was more upset than she was. Once again she felt that hot surging impulse to touch him. Something about his strength and poise always seemed to churn up a trembling weakness in her whenever she saw him. Now, recalling his words to her yesterday about knowing how to treat his own son, she could guess that he was embarrassed about today's mix-up. More than that, however, he was genuinely anxious. He was still dressed for business, but had thrown off his coat and loosened his tie. He hurried over to her.

"Rennie, is Scott—"

"He's here. Right around the corner of the house and very busy," Rennie explained. She saw his broad shoulders relax.

"I was sure you'd have him with you," he said in a rush. "I wasn't really worried. It's just that Dad and I got our messages crossed. I thought he was going to pick up Scott, and he thought I was."

"Take a look," Rennie said, and walked with him to the corner of the house, where on a small flag-stoned area an unhappy Pete was standing in a tub of soapy water while Scott scrubbed and soothed.

"Hi, Dad!" Scott called out happily. "Boy, this dog sure did need a bath. I'm going to hose him down now."

"That's his towel on the bench," Rennie said.

"Okay. Hey, you really goofed up, didn't you, Dad?" he teased cheerfully.

Connor shot a swift look at Rennie. "Afraid I did, son." He hesitated, squinting into the late-afternoon sun. His nearness was a tangible thing, its warmth something she could feel along her own nerves and skin. Surreptitiously she inched away from him. "I'm sorry," he said then, looking down at her with a heart-melting smile.

"Really, I was glad to bring him home with me," she murmured.

"Not about that." He shook his head. "I gave you a hard time yesterday just because some girl had beaned him on the head. If that's the worst that ever happens to him—"

"Just forget it. I have."

They moved away from Scott. "And then I acted so damned stuffy," he went on, rubbing the back of his neck, "about knowing what was best for my son. Well, I still think I do, but this business of being a full-time father—it's a new role for me."

"You shouldn't worry about it," Rennie said. "He's a great kid and you're doing fine. By the end of the summer you're going to be sorry it's over, and you'll be feeling pretty proud of yourself."

"End of the summer?" He frowned and his blue eyes narrowed slightly. "He's not leaving at the end of the summer. I have full custody of him now. He's staying with me."

Rennie caught her breath with surprise. "Oh, I'm sorry. I thought— Well, I just assumed..."

He looked away. "And it's a big responsibility, as I'm beginning to realize. I really want him with me, but I don't feel very well prepared."

"You're doing fine," Rennie repeated in a soft voice. "Just relax and enjoy him."

The blue eyes returned to her, searching her face as if he hoped to find some answer there. Rennie could feel a melting deep inside her, a tremulous response to the look. Then there was a sudden shout from the patio. Connor and Rennie hurried back just as Scott succeeded in wrapping a large beach towel around Pete. The corgi peered out dolefully from its folds.

"He sprayed me when he shook," Scott explained.

"Well done." Rennie laughed. "I'm hiring you as my permanent dog washer."

"And now that that's done," Connor said, "let's get out of Miss Tate's hair, Scott. Time we went home and gave her a chance to recover."

Scott clutched the dog with a stricken expression, his glance darting from one adult to the other. "But I'm invited for dinner, Dad! Miss Tate said I could stay."

Rennie saw faint color wash into Connor's face as he turned to her. "That was really kind of you, Rennie. Perhaps another time—"

"No, not another time," Rennie insisted. "The invitation stands, and you're invited too. There's plenty." The moment the words were out, she experienced the fluttering unsure sensation again. What was she letting herself in for? But she added, "That is, unless it would upset some plans of your own." She had a sudden vision of an elegant restaurant and a beautifully dressed woman clinging to his arm.

"Oh, hey, that's neat! Can we, Dad?"

Connor's gaze returned to Rennie, slightly confused. He lifted his shoulders in a gesture of helplessness and said, "If it won't upset anything and if you're sure you don't mind having us, we'd be happy to stay."

"Great!" Scott shouted.

"Then you'd better take Pete for a walk so he can finish drying off," Rennie said. "Once around the block ought to do it. It's either that or the hair dryer, and I'll tell you right now he hates that dryer. Here's his leash in case you need it."

"Is there something I can do to help?" Connor asked.

Rennie hesitated for only a moment, thinking what it would be like, the two of them close together, moving around the little kitchen, his nearness making her light-headed. Then she said quickly, "Not a thing. You go along on the walk. Scott has a lot of news to tell you."

He shot her a look that was half curious, half reluctant, and as the two walked down the driveway with the damp dog between them, Rennie could hear the little boy's eager voice starting on its recital. "Randolph and me, we found this cat, see—Randolph's this guy I met—and he looked real hungry, the cat, I mean, so Randolph and me, we went to the store and got cat food. Only then Miss Tate said it wasn't a he at all. It was a she, and Randolph's grandma said she might have kittens...."

Rennie turned and went back to the vegetables she'd been slicing for the pasta primavera. Then she pulled the dropleaf table away from the wall, extended the leaves and laid three place mats on it. She felt a strange and unfamiliar excitement as she did all the ordinary things involved in preparing the meal, thinking how she was doing it for *him*.

It was amazing, Rennie thought as she looked across the table at Connor when they sat down to dinner. He appeared totally at ease here in her little rented house. She knew he must be accustomed to the most exclusive restaurants, and she had no doubt he demanded impeccable service. Also, she was fairly sure she was right about the beautiful woman she'd pictured on his arm. Men of wealth and power were never without that kind of adornment. Yet here at her grandmother Tate's dropleaf table, he gave no indication of being other than completely at home.

Scott was more open about his feelings.

"This is a great house, isn't it, Dad?"

"'Great' is exactly the word I'd have picked. And it suits Miss Tate, doesn't it?"

"Please let's drop the 'Miss Tate' business."

His eyebrows went up. "But you're a teacher. Teachers deserve respect."

"Well, I'm not a teacher when I'm home."

"Then can I call you Rennie like Dad does?" Scott asked.

"Only when we're by ourselves," Connor answered before she could. "Remember that."

Scott grinned, obviously enjoying the conspiracy. Connor asked Rennie with mock seriousness, "Well, now. What kind of trouble did the kid get into today?"

"No trouble at all. You've already heard, haven't you? An errand of mercy. Cat rescue, that is. And his garden plot's coming along beautifully."

"Mr. Steele brought cookies," Scott announced. "And you know what? He *made* them himself."

"That bread is his, too," Rennie said, nodding toward the golden-crusted slices in a basket. "Mr. Steele used to be the chief baker when the old bakery was in business. It was quite an operation then."

"I remember it," Connor said. "Do you?" His eyes stayed on her with a concentration that Rennie found disconcerting, yet inside her was a glowing center of warmth. It was of course preposterous, she reminded herself. His interest in her was a reflection of his preoccupation with Scott. He was, in reality, a new father, diving into responsibilities he hadn't known before, and he simply found her a help, saw her as an ally.

"Goodness, yes," she replied, feeling tongue-tied. "It was really the center of the neighborhood. Dozens of local people worked there."

"So what happened?"

"A bigger bakery chain bought it out. Took what they needed in the way of equipment, then closed it down. An old story, I'm afraid. So now we have to eat mass-produced bread from an out-of-town bakery, unless we're lucky enough to have Mr. Steele bake for us now and then."

Connor reached for another slice. "Mr. Steele is an artist, I can see that. And so are you. This meal is delicious."

Rennie felt herself blush and looked down at her plate.

When they'd finished he insisted on helping her with the dishes.

"Oh, no, really. I can do them later in no time," she insisted.

"Wouldn't hear of it. Wash or dry? You pick."

Rennie, who was certain he'd never washed a dish in his life, shook her head helplessly and handed him a towel.

"And how about one for Scott? He ate as much as I did." His blue eyes sparkled as he said it and seemed to explore her face as if storing it away in memory.

"We'd be tripping over each other." She laughed. "There's not enough room. But I have another job for Scott. Here." She handed the boy a brush. "I always groom Pete's coat after a bath."

"Oh, great! Come on, Pete." Boy and dog hopped onto the couch and began the operation.

For a few moments Rennie concentrated on the matter of the dishes. She was intensely aware of Connor's nearness. She was aware also of the way she must look. Why hadn't she taken an extra minute to put on something a bit more appealing than these old cutoffs and a baggy T-shirt? She was entirely too offhand about her appearance, that was her trouble. Well, one of her troubles. Connor was used to well-groomed women who knew how to throw together coordinated outfits—

"You look absolutely captivating, you know that?" he said suddenly.

She whirled around. "Were you reading my thoughts? I was just thinking I should— Oh, never mind."

"I'm just not used to women like you," he said. His gaze still hovered on her as if he couldn't get enough.

Rennie tried to bring her thoughts back to earth. Of course he wasn't used to women like her. A novelty, that was all she was.

"Tell me a little about yourself," he said, picking up an iced-tea glass and polishing it carefully. "You said you knew the South Street neighborhood well."

"I grew up there." Rennie plunged her hands back into the soapy water. "Well, on the edge of it. My parents were both schoolteachers, and as far back as I can remember, our house was always full. Anytime there was a problem—with anybody in the neighborhood—it was our house they always came to."

"And are they still there, your parents?"

"No, they've moved to the West Coast. I have a sister out there, in Seattle. They wanted me to go with them, but I'd just got the job at East Side Elementary and, I don't know, I like it here in Palmer City. Except I feel sorry for what's happened to the old neighborhood."

"You're making a difference there, though."

"Only a small difference," she said, wondering if she sounded bitter.

He changed the subject. "Actually I hadn't been here in Palmer City for several years. Not to really live here."

"Where were you?" She kept her eyes on the soapy water, trying not to be so aware of his nearness.

"Oh, different places. Away at school and college, to start with. Then some time in California, some in Arizona—lots of building going on out there. But when Dad decided to retire and Mom died, I figured it was time to come home. Then I got the idea of doing over that block on Berkeley Street and moving in there. Of course Dad never really retired. He just pared a huge business down to a one-man operation and kept right at it."

"He told me how much he loves gardening."

They went on working, and Rennie was surprised to find that conversation began to come more easily, although it was obvious that Connor was avoiding any mention of his marriage. When Rennie put the last dish away and Connor hung up his towel, she glanced

into the living room and then tapped him on the arm
to draw his attention. Boy and dog had both fallen
asleep in what looked like total comfort.

Connor's arm slid around her waist as they observed the scene together, and Rennie stayed perfectly
still, trying not to react even though she could feel the
world spin around her again.

"Can we sit out there?" he asked in a low voice,
motioning toward the screen door that led to the
backyard.

She nodded, and they went out together. It was the
same small flagged area where Scott had washed the
dog, but with the tub put away and the hose coiled out
of sight, it looked like a different spot completely. A
profusion of shrubs and flowers, all white, grew
around its rim, gleaming softly in the darkness.

"It's my white garden," Rennie explained. "Because I'm not here much in the daytime, and I wanted
something I could enjoy at night. So I planted everything white. Nicotiana—that's what smells so good—
and daisies, white impatiens. That silvery stuff's ar-
temisia. I sit out here a lot." She led the way to a bench
at one side, and they sat together.

"What a great idea," he said. "I'm going to have to
tell Dad about it."

"Oh, it won't be news to him. I'll bet he's planted
white gardens himself."

They were quiet for a moment, listening to the gentle night sounds around them and presently to the
thump and whir of an air conditioner going on somewhere nearby.

"I didn't think it was that warm," he said.

"That's Mrs. Bridgewater, my landlady," Rennie
explained. "She lives in the big house over there." She

pointed to the left. "She's probably just giving the unit a trial run, getting ready for real summer weather. By the sound of it, she'll be calling me any day now to come over and have a look at it."

"Really?"

She could feel his eyes on her, staring curiously.

"Oh, sure. I'm also good at furnace repair, and I do a little carpentry."

"You're kidding!"

"No, I'm not. I get a good chunk knocked off the rent for it."

He went on staring. "You really are amazing."

The sleek well-coiffed women she had been imagining earlier filled her mind's eyes again, and she thought wryly that she would gladly trade "amazing" for a more glamorous description. "Actually, the way I grew up, it isn't so amazing," she said. "My parents believed in self-reliance and doing things yourself."

"Nothing wrong with that."

"No." But there had been times when she'd wished for someone to lean on. Just for a moment. She'd had the feeling the night she'd met Connor at the garden site and the sudden thunder had caused him to hold her against him. For a second she'd known the blissful wonder of being cared for, looked after. Even though she treasured her independence, loved her self-sufficiency, there were times...

"Do you know what I was thinking in there just now—when I saw Scott sleeping?" he asked.

"I can imagine. You were thinking how great it is to be a father."

"Maybe that, subconsciously. But mostly I was thinking how Lisa, my wife, never wanted him."

Rennie turned to him. "Oh, no. I can't believe that."

"It's true, I'm afraid. But I blame myself more than her, because I was all caught up in work and I never paid enough attention to either of them. Oh, I made sure we got back here for Christmases with Mom and Dad, although Lisa hated that. I guess the chemistry between the two of us was all wrong from the start. After we were divorced I really threw myself into work, and all the time I told myself that he was being cared for, that he'd be all right with his mother. But deep down I knew he wasn't. He had nursemaids and then private schools and all that, but nothing real. No real family. I saw him summers, brought him here to my folks' house, but that was because I felt guilty."

"Well, you have him now. And you mustn't feel guilty. It's a fresh start. Everything brand-new. Didn't your wife, er, ex-wife, object when you sued for custody?"

He shook his head. "She's got another husband now and a new life. It wasn't that she was a bad mother exactly. It's just that she never gave herself a chance to know Scott. Maybe some women aren't cut out for motherhood."

Rennie was quiet for a moment, thinking of the unknown Lisa and how much she'd lost. Thinking, too, how much Connor had left out of the story—all the pain and anguish this failed marriage must have cost him.

"Hey, I've got an idea," he said. "Let's go to the seashore this weekend. The three of us. And Pete, of course. We'll drive up to Gull Island beach and make a day of it. I'll bring the lunch. It's my turn."

Rennie was too surprised to answer at first. Then she said, trying to keep her voice even, "Are you sure? I mean, do you really want to?"

"More than anything." He leaned toward her. "How about it, Miss Tate?" And before she could answer he had brought his mouth down to cover hers in a kiss that made Rennie's toes curl. His arms were around her in that strong sheltering embrace that felt so right to her. Only this kiss was different from the brash impulsive one he had given her when they'd stood together in her living room. This one was deeper, fiercer, more demanding. What was she doing making a bargain with a man like Connor Blackstone? Rennie thought in a kind of desperation. How could it be anything but one-sided? Where would it all lead and who would be hurt? Yet as she leaned into the kiss, returning it wildly, her heart answered with perverse conviction: *It doesn't matter. It doesn't matter.*

CHAPTER FIVE

THE NEXT DAY the mercury climbed into the high eighties. Rennie brought two bowls to the garden, one for the cat's food and one for the water. The children took turns seeing that they were kept filled. Seedlings wilted. The gardeners were kept busy lugging sprinkling cans back and forth from the faucet next door. Mr. Steele, working tirelessly in his corner of the lot, brought paint and brushes, and when he'd finished his stint of planting and watering for the day, started sprucing up the rickety shed, helped by the children, who slathered on the paint with eager strokes.

Around midafternoon, Teddy Pohl came running to fetch Rennie. "Miss Tate, come see what Mr. Steele's done!"

Rennie followed him back to the corner and then stood there in silent admiration. The shed had been painted red, and once the quick-drying paint was firm, Mr. Steele had painted a window in white. And not just an ordinary window, but an open window with a horse peering out. The horse was still incomplete; Mr. Steele was only outlining it when Rennie came up to the admiring group.

"Mr. Steele! That's wonderful!" she exclaimed. "Just what we needed to make the place look like a real farm."

"Don't have the colors I need to finish," he said modestly. "I'll bring 'em tomorrow."

"I never dreamed you had so many talents," Rennie told him. "Randolph, go get your grandma to come and look."

Randolph sprinted off, but in a moment Rennie heard his frightened cry. "Miss Tate, Miss Tate, come quick!"

Rennie dashed after him and found Callie lying on her side in the path, her straw hat askew, her handkerchief clutched in her hand.

"Grandma!" Randolph cried.

"Now, child, I'm all right," Callie said weakly. "Just lost my balance for a minute is all."

"Randolph, tell Mr. Steele to come here," Rennie ordered as she helped the older woman to a sitting position. "You've been out in the sun too long, Callie. Now just sit quiet."

And when Mr. Steele hurried up, Rennie explained the matter to him and added, "I'll take her over to the clinic in the next block. Randolph, you come with me. Mr. Steele, if you'd just keep an eye on little Donald till we get back. The others'll be fine. Becky'll help you. Tell Scott to look after Pete."

Donald had by now spotted his grandmother. Frightened, he started to howl. Becky, coming up behind him, murmured reassurances, then picked him up, lugged him back to the shed and stuck a paintbrush in his hand.

"Ain't a thing in the world wrong with me," Callie protested as Rennie and Mr. Steele helped her to the pickup.

"I'm sure there isn't," Rennie said. "But we're going to let Dr. Gomez have a look at you anyway. Hop in, Randolph.'' The older boy, she knew, was just as frightened as Donald was, but in a more grown-up way, and she thought it would reassure him to come with them.

The storefront clinic had been operating for two years on a shoestring budget, relying on citizen contributions, government grants and a small allowance from the city. Marguerita Gomez, whom everyone called Daisy, had been in college with Rennie before going on to medical school. Tiny and efficient, she hustled Callie quickly into a curtained-off examining room as soon as they arrived, while Rennie sat with Randolph.

"Grandma's pretty old," the boy said worriedly.

"That doesn't mean a thing," Rennie soothed, hoping she was right.

Dr. Gomez emerged moments later. "Mrs. Burgess is fine," she said cheerfully. "Her blood pressure is slightly elevated, and I think I'll recommend some medication for that. It's not really high enough to worry about, though. What got to her was just that hot sun, I'm sure."

Callie came up behind her, smoothing her cotton dress and straightening her hat. "Well, I ain't gonna stop working in that garden, tell you right now."

Daisy Gomez looked to Rennie for help. "Rennie, can this lady garden in the shade?"

"We'll arrange something," Rennie said firmly.

That afternoon when she got home she went out to the cavernous old building that had once been a barn and now served as a garage for Mrs. Bridgewater's ancient Cadillac. She rummaged through the piles of three-legged chairs, defunct toasters, ornate picture frames, rump-sprung sofas and broken bridge lamps that shared space with the old car, banging about and raising dust until Mrs. Bridgewater herself appeared in the doorway.

"Is that you, Rennie? What in the world are you looking for?" Mrs. Bridgewater, who still wore a hair net and white gloves to go to the supermarket, was a sprightly old lady of seventy-nine who had been born in the same house she now occupied.

"I'm sure I saw a wooden lawn chair here once," Rennie said, blowing her hair away from her forehead. "The kind with a bracket on the back for holding an umbrella."

"Oh, yes. We called those Adirondack chairs. Mr. Bridgewater, my late husband, used to sit in it. Well, it must be around here somewhere. Why do you want it?"

"I'd like to buy it from you, if you're not sentimentally attached to it or anything," Rennie said, and went on to explain what had happened to Callie.

"Oh, my word. Poor soul." Mrs. Bridgewater's face drew into lines of concern. "You don't have to buy it. I'll gladly donate it. The chair's a real antique, I believe. Now wait, isn't that it back of the sewing machine? And the umbrella that goes with it should be there, too. Wait, I'll give you a hand."

Pushing and tugging, they managed to free the chair, and Rennie dragged it outside.

"Doesn't look too bad," she said. "I'll scrub it down. Now let's see about the umbrella."

Mrs. Bridgewater, wearing large rubber gloves, insisted on helping with the cleanup, and within minutes the old-fashioned chair sat in the driveway, free of dust and its big umbrella firmly attached.

"Perfect!" Rennie said. "Take it off your income tax as a donation, Mrs. B."

The old lady laughed delightedly. "Wonderful idea—I'll do that." She straightened and cocked her head. "Isn't that your phone I hear?"

Rennie dashed inside, drying her hands on her shorts, and snatched up the receiver.

"Hi. I was beginning to be afraid you weren't home."

Rennie could feel her mouth going dry and her legs going weak. She sat down in a chair.

"I was outside in the driveway. Mrs. Bridgewater and I were cleaning up a chair and an umbrella."

"Planning to sit out in the rain?" His teasing voice caressed her. Rennie cradled the phone close as if to draw him nearer, but she tried to keep her own voice light.

"No, silly. It's a sun chair."

"Well, it sounds as if there's a story to go with that, but right now all I wanted to do was to talk to you and mention in passing that Saturday seems awfully far away."

"It's the day after tomorrow!"

"As I say—light-years."

Suddenly it seemed so to Rennie, too. Endless time before she saw him again. "It'll be here before you know it," she said, not meaning it.

"Well, possibly." She could picture his frown, mock serious, as he considered it. "But by way of speeding things along, why don't we have dinner together tonight?"

"Tonight?" she echoed.

"Right away."

"Oh, but I..." Rennie looked down at herself in dismay, taking in the dust from the garage, the dirt from the garden. "I'm not dressed or anything. I'm mean, I'm not cleaned up yet."

"We won't go anyplace fancy. How about the Montgomery House? Just wash your face—you'll look beautiful."

"The Montgomery—"

"I'll be there in an hour. Or maybe half an hour. I'm just a little way up the interstate."

"You're calling from your car? Oh, dear, I don't think I can possibly—"

The phone went dead. For a moment Rennie stared at it. Then, galvanized into action, she dashed for the shower. Moments later, wrapped in the terry robe and wielding the hair dryer, she began frantically going over the possibilities in her meager wardrobe. The Montgomery House might not be Connor Blackstone's idea of "anyplace fancy," but Rennie had never even set foot in it. It was just outside of town, a huge old Greek Revival house converted into a restaurant, and its stately pillared front looked out over sweeping green lawns and spreading trees. Even without having seen its interior, Rennie could picture dark polished floors, heavy white linen, attentive waiters. This was definitely not your local fast-food hangout. And it had been so long since she'd been anywhere requiring more than a clean T-shirt that she hardly knew where to turn to find anything suitable.

She fluffed her short dark hair with a brush, turned off the dryer and hurried to her closet, assessing the contents with dismay. White pants. She did have those. And white pants could go almost anywhere in summer. But the Montgomery House? She bit her lip and went on looking. Far back at the end of the rack was a white eyelet dress she'd never worn. Estelle, her married sister, had sent it from Mexico when she and Ed had gone there on vacation the previous year. Rennie drew it out. An off-the-shoulder neckline with a wide ruffle. A narrow waist with a full flounced skirt. She'd always loved its simplicity but had never found the right place to wear it. And red sandals—she had red sandals here somewhere. Quickly she made the decision and started dressing.

Her heart was racing as she stood in front of the mirror moments later. What would he say? How would she look to him? And then suddenly, in a more sobering vein, was she making a terrible mistake about all this? She stopped turning this way and that and stood quite still, her hands clasped together, staring at the other Rennie in the full-length mirror on the closet door. What possible future could there be in a relationship with a man like Connor Blackstone? She lived in a world very different from his. No doubt she was unlike any of the women he'd gone out with up to now, but once that novelty wore off, what interest would he have in her? Didn't the attraction have more to do with Scott, anyway, than with her? Connor was anxious to do the right thing where his son was concerned, and she and Scott seemed to hit it off well....

Rennie's teeth caught her lower lip to keep it from trembling just as the doorbell rang.

Pete let out a sharp bark and ran to his guard position. Rennie shut the closet door and followed him, hesitating for a fraction of a second to square her shoulders before opening the door.

He stood there looking even handsomer than she'd remembered in a navy jacket and light gray trousers. His face registered surprise as his eyes swept over her.

"I'm sorry. I must have the wrong place. I'm looking for a very efficient teacher, a Miss Tate, who repairs air conditioners and furnaces and generally has a great deal of garden dirt under her nails."

Rennie's eyes locked with his as she slowly held out both hands for his inspection. "You have the right place," she said. "It's just that it's a different Miss Tate." Her voice sounded small and distant even to her own ears.

"It must be," he agreed soberly, clasping both her hands. "The Miss Tate I know isn't fifteen. Which is about how old you look in that dress."

"Oh dear." She frowned anxiously. "I didn't mean to—"

"Darling Rennie," he said with a smile. "What a worrier you are. Most of the women I know would kill to be able to manage such a look. That's Mexican, isn't it?"

"Yes. My sister sent it to me. It's a wedding dress, she told me. Or, that is, it might be. I mean, not necessarily of course." Rennie blushed.

His eyes sparkled with enjoyment. "Of course," he said. "Now, are we ready?"

Rennie swallowed hard and nodded.

Without ever having seen the interior of the Montgomery House, she'd imagined it with dead-on accuracy. The dark polished floors, the heavy white linen, the elegant candlelit table settings, the fresh flowers, the white-coated waiters. The maître d' greeted Connor by name and said they'd reserved his usual table.

"Good evening, miss," he said to her, and Rennie managed to answer him.

Only a few other tables were occupied as they sat down, and Rennie leaned across to whisper, "Are we a little early?"

"Actually we are. That's because I was anxious. I have this awful habit of not liking to wait for something I want." His eyes caught hers and held them.

When the waiter came with menus, Connor said, "I think we'll have some champagne to start. Would that suit you?" And when Rennie nodded wordlessly, he made a selection from the wine list. "Now then," he said when the waiter had gone. "Explain the chair with the umbrella, please. Is this to take to the beach on Saturday?"

Rennie laughed. She was still not feeling completely at ease in this place, so it wasn't a wholehearted laugh. "Goodness no," she said. "It's for Randolph's grandmother, Callie Burgess."

"Randolph. Now let's see. He's Scott's new friend who has a half-interest in the cat."

"Right. And his grandmother is a delightful lady who comes to the garden every day. Only today, I think, was too hot for her." Briefly she explained what had happened. "Since she absolutely refuses to give up the garden, Daisy says she'll have to stay in the shade."

"Daisy?" His eyebrows shot up.

"Well, it's Dr. Gomez actually. She's in charge of the South Street Clinic in the next block. That's where I took Callie."

"I see. So the chair is for Callie."

"Right. She can sit in it whenever she feels the need to rest and still keep an eye on the boys and do a little gardening from time to time."

"Was that your idea?" His eyes were fastened on her face, scanning it tenderly.

"Well, yes. Mrs. Bridgewater helped, though, and she's going to make it a donation. When I suggested she could make it tax deductible, I think I made her day."

He tipped back his head and laughed heartily just as the waiter returned with champagne, tulip glasses and ice bucket. "Could I hire you to give me a hand with interesting suggestions like that when tax time rolls around again?"

Rennie smiled back at him. The waiter poured their wine and left. Connor raised his glass. "To new friends," he said quietly.

"New friends," Rennie murmured, then took a sip. She hadn't tasted champagne since her sister's wedding. And Estelle and Ed had been married—how long?

"What's indicated by that thoughtful look?" he asked.

"I was just trying to remember how long it's been since I had champagne," she admitted. "I'm afraid it's about six years."

"Then I'm glad you're having it with me," he said. "Makes it an occasion."

"What about Scott?" she asked. "What's he doing this evening?"

"Oh, he and Dad are baching it together. Dining at Burger King, I believe, and then Dad's rented *Fantasia*."

Just for a moment, Rennie wished she and Connor were doing that. The Montgomery House was old and beautiful and its elegance was of the understated kind, typical of this coastal Southern city, yet it was still hard for her to feel she belonged there. She knew she could handle any situation she found herself in, but she'd been quite content in her vastly different world, and she couldn't help feeling slightly out of place in this one.

"Get it out of your head right now," he said with a smile. "You're the prettiest woman in this room and don't you forget it."

"Are you a mind reader?" she asked in genuine astonishment. But she experienced a rush of warmth all the same at the reminder that she was with *him*. Whatever she thought about the surroundings he lived in, as long as they were together, the two of them made a world of their own. She could actually feel it folding around her, warm and protective. He put his hand out and closed it over hers on the table.

"Connor! Darling!" A woman had arrived at their table on a cloud of expensive scent before either of them noticed.

"Jilly, hello," he said, half-rising.

"Oh, sit down, please. I won't disturb you. Do go on enjoying your champagne. It looks like a real party." She slanted a quick look at Rennie, and Rennie managed a weak smile.

"Jillian Brooks, Rennie Tate," Connor said.

"Oh, so *you're* the fabulous Miss Tate," Jillian Brooks said. She was tall and blond and willowy, with slim legs she showed off to their best advantage in a short white skirt with a long black jacket. Her pale hair was pulled black loosely and fastened with a black-and-white scarf. A heavy gold bracelet encircled one narrow wrist.

Rennie blinked at the blatantly social lie. "Not fabulous, really."

"Nonsense. I should have recognized you. We all saw your picture in the paper," Jillian said. "And here you are, dining with the cruel landowner."

"I'm fairly civilized, Jilly," Connor protested.

Rennie felt uncomfortable with their banter. She kept her determined smile in place, but she knew, somehow, that Jillian Brooks was not a friend.

"I won't keep you," Jillian said. "Just wanted to check to make sure you didn't forget about Saturday, Connor."

"Saturday?" His eyebrows shot up.

"How like you! You *have* forgotten. It's the cocktail party at Madge Preston's. For the civic symphony? In her garden, if the weather's fine."

"Damn. I'm sorry, Jilly, I'm afraid I did forget. But I'll send my usual check to the symphony. You know that's all they really want."

Rennie saw Jillian's pale eyes narrow with anger, then change back to flippant nonconcern in the space of seconds.

"Aren't you the hard-bitten cynic, though. Well, if it turns out you can make it, after all, you know where we'll all be."

"Not likely, I'm afraid," he said. "We're going to Gull Island beach—Rennie, Scott and I."

"The beach! How marvelous. Didn't know anyone *went* to the beach anymore. Anyway, I'll be off. Have a good time, you two."

"Thank you," Rennie murmured.

He shook his head slightly when she'd left. "Jilly's quite harmless," he said. "A bit of an airhead, really."

Rennie took a sip of champagne. "She smelled pretty good."

He put his head back and laughed in a way that showed the strong lines of his throat. The gesture was becoming familiar to her and caused her a slight tremor each time she saw it. He kept his eyes on her face, studying her as though he couldn't get enough.

They ate and talked their way through red snapper cooked with shallots and white wine, tiny new potatoes served in their jackets and Caesar salad. The dining room filled up rapidly and before long was noisy with conversation. Jillian Brooks, Rennie saw, was at a table across the room with a party of six. Rennie noticed that her eyes returned frequently to their table.

"How about a crème brûlée to finish off?" Connor asked. "They do it beautifully here."

Rennie took a deep breath. "I shouldn't, but okay. I'll run an extra block tomorrow morning. I haven't had crème brûlée since France."

"And when was that?"

"Just before my senior year in college. Four of us went. Strictly economy class. Nothing but a backpack for luggage. The kind of thing you never dream of doing once you arrive at the age of reason."

"I wish I'd known you then," he said softly.

Rennie smiled at him but didn't answer. It was almost enough to be near him, to enjoy the warm caressing looks he lavished on her, but she couldn't keep a certain down-to-earth part of her mind from wondering where this was all going. Did he really mean the things he said? What exactly was she to him? He was a man who could obviously have his pick of any one of the elegant women in this room. Was she anything more than merely a novelty to him? This kind of reasoning went on in her mind, but it was far less compelling than the lightning-quick thrill that shuddered through her when he touched her hand or slipped his arm around her waist. Reactions like that could be dangerous, because there was no way of arguing with them, no confronting them with logic.

Suddenly she was fearful that everything she was thinking was showing on her face.

"You order the dessert," she said. "I'll just duck into the ladies' room for a minute."

He nodded and rose as she left.

An elderly woman with a cane was just approaching the door of the powder room as Rennie got there.

"Wait. Let me help you," Rennie said quickly, and held the door open for her.

"Oh, thank you, dear. That's very kind," the woman said. As she slowly entered, Rennie could hear a scrap of conversation going on out of sight behind the open door.

"...a really appalling little dress. Sort of like the one I wore to my high-school prom."

"Connor always did like the sweet girlish types—for a while."

"Mmm. This one's more of a back-to-the-soil peasant type."

"Novelty, that's all. You can't tell me..."

Rennie stepped into the room and saw Jillian Brooks and another woman at the mirror. Both of them spotted her reflection in the glass and fell silent. Then Jillian made a recovery and said, "Oh, hi there, Rennie. This is Madge Preston."

The other woman, a fortyish redhead, gave her a cold unabashed smile. "The garden lady, right? I'll bet you could give us all some pointers. Sometimes my garden just gets so tired looking."

Rennie could feel herself shaking inwardly with anger, but she kept her poise. "It's all in the soil," she said pleasantly. "You need to keep mulching." She gave Jillian Brooks a challenging look. "And of course plenty of manure."

The shaking had not entirely subsided when she got back to the table. The mirror in the ladies' room had already told her she'd gone pale under her tan. He got up as she approached, and his smile faded to a look of concern.

"Something wrong?" he asked quickly. His gaze moved to the two women who were just returning to their own table across the room.

"No, nothing." She sat down, willing herself into composure.

"Encounter in the ladies'?"

"It was nothing," she insisted.

He was quiet for a few moments while the waiter brought their desserts. Then he said gently, "You mustn't mind people like Jilly and Madge, if that's what it is. If they...said something, I mean. The world's full of women like that, but they haven't a thing to do with us. And Rennie, you'd fit in anywhere."

"Not fitting in doesn't bother me," she said bluntly. "Being talked down to—*that* ticks me off a little." She took a deep breath. "Hey, they're just...different from the people I'm used to, that's all." She heard her own voice sounding stiff from her effort at maintaining control.

"Would you like to leave?" he asked quietly.

Some of the color flowed back into Rennie's face. "I certainly would not. I haven't had my dessert yet."

On the way home in the soft darkness of the summer evening, he asked her again what had happened, and at last, reluctantly, she told him, skimming over it briefly and now able to pass it off with a grin. The reply she'd given made him hoot with laughter.

"I don't know why I was worried about you," he said, shaking his head as he maneuvered the car down her street and into the driveway. "I'm sure you could take care of yourself in a cage full of Bengal tigers."

"Hardly," she murmured. But the unpleasant incident seemed far away. Reality was now—this moment beside him in the dark leather interior of his car. Only a small lingering uneasiness remained as she heard the echo of the brittle words: *Connor always did like the sweet girlish types—for a while.* Rennie spoke suddenly to scatter the memory.

"Will you come in for a few minutes?"

"I thought you'd never ask."

The heat had eased, and a small breeze had sprung up. A nearly full moon lit their way. She saw how it silvered his tall frame, catching in his hair, changing him from the daytime businessman into something more primitive and otherworldly. He'd removed his tie and left his jacket in the car, and she could feel the warmth from his body through his shirt.

Pete was at the door, bustling and eager to greet them.

"I'm afraid all I have is iced tea," Rennie apologized. "Too much of a letdown after champagne?"

"Iced tea will be fine," he said. While she went to the tiny kitchen to get it, he strolled to the player in the corner and began looking over the stack of CDs. He slipped one on, and mellow music filled the little house.

"Can we sit outside?" he called to her.

"Good idea." She put the glasses on a tray and he held the back door open for her. The music floated through the screen. Pete, who'd followed them outside, dashed off into the shadows, sniffing and investigating.

"You're like a part of your white garden tonight," Connor said as she bent to put the tray on a small wrought-iron table. But when she started to sit on the bench he caught her hand and pulled her to him, slipping an arm around her and starting to move slowly with the music. Rennie said nothing, but let her head rest against his shoulder as they danced in the moonlight on the tiny stone patio.

"You're a wonder-worker, you know that?" he whispered. His breath caressed her hair when he spoke.

She shook her head. Her lips pressed against his chest through his shirt.

"Well, you are. I hear it from Scott every day. He's so full of talk about you and the others. Before this I could never get him to open his mouth."

"You may live to regret it."

He held her closer. "You're something special, Miss Rennie Tate. I think I knew it that very first day when you stood there in those big work shoes giving me hell about the trash."

"And I was trying to fake you out, pretending I knew Connor Blackstone. I wasn't too smart, was I?"

"You were adorable. And the next day, too, when the tractor wouldn't start. I couldn't believe my eyes when I saw you riding that thing."

"That truck driver was beginning to make me nervous."

"I don't think anything really makes you nervous for long."

"He was pretty big, though."

He laughed close to her ear, and she looked up at him. Quickly, before she could lower her head again, he bent and caught her lips in his own. They stood still, drenched in moonlight, with the white garden throwing a ring of summer enchantment around them. Rennie felt a fevered stirring inside her, a longing to let the moment go on and on, a certainty that right now, tonight, she could give herself to this man without thinking twice.

The voice broke through her thoughts, acid and insistent: *Connor always did like the sweet girlish types—for a while.* She stiffened and pulled away from the kiss. His raised eyebrows asked her what was wrong.

"Maybe we'd better have that iced tea now," she said.

They went to the bench and sat. Raising his glass, he drank and then looked at her over the rim. "I haven't figured you out yet, I'm afraid. But I'm not going to stop trying."

"Suit yourself," she said teasingly. "Now tell me about Saturday. What time do we leave?"

"The earlier the better. How about nine?"

"Okay. But let me bring something."

"Nope. I said it was my party. Scott and I'll take care of it." He put his glass down and slid a hand out to cover hers on the bench. "I'm not trying to rush you, you know."

If he only knew how much I want to be rushed, she thought. *If only I could be more sure.* If, if, if. In spite of her reservations, she felt herself leaning toward

him, toward the strong arms that moved around her
again. This time she raised her face to him, and his kiss
was a flame that seared through her. She tasted it, returned it, let her fingers tangle themselves in his hair.
And when the insistent voice returned to her, she deliberately turned a deaf ear, not caring what danger it
warned of.

CHAPTER SIX

RENNIE DELIBERATELY kept herself busy on Friday. She brought the old chair to the garden in the back of her pickup and, with Mr. Steele to help her, set it up for Callie.

"I declare," Callie kept saying, "I'm settin' here just like the Queen of England. If that ain't the prettiest!"

Rennie was relieved to see that the older woman was looking quite herself again, but she still checked on her from time to time during the day. Scott and Randolph looked after "their" cat, and now and then Scott shot Rennie a conspiratorial glance to remind her of the secret they shared about tomorrow.

The garden itself was becoming greener, all the plots bursting with lush new growth. Mr. Steele's refurbished shed now had its painted horse peering out of the painted window. Some of the workmen from the building next door strolled over at noon and asked if they could eat lunch there. When Rennie agreed, they sat in the shade of the shed with Mr. Steele, and when they were finished, carefully picked up every scrap of trash before leaving. Rennie was growing used to them and to the racket they made; she scarcely noticed the noise of the power saw and the steady hammering that went on all day.

Rennie discussed with her gardeners the relative merits of staking tomatoes versus enclosing them in wire cages. There was considerable interest in the cages, but stakes, as she pointed out, would cost nothing, since the workmen would certainly be agreeable to furnishing odds and ends of lumber for them. Teddy Pohl's Green Wonder bean was growing at an astonishing rate, and Teddy himself, Rennie noticed, was growing along with it. He had a healthy tan, and the stiff blue jeans he'd appeared in that first day were already softening and fading.

"Will your dad be picking you up this afternoon?" she asked Scott as the shadows began to lengthen and the gardeners started to leave.

"No, he's got to go to some meeting. I'm going home with Grandpa."

Rennie kept her disappointment hidden. It didn't matter, she reminded herself sensibly. She had last night, and the memory of his arms around her in the white garden. And tomorrow... The whole glorious day stretched ahead of them. She took a deep breath and waved the boy off when the Blackstone Landscaping truck pulled up for him.

Even so, she found it hard to contemplate going home by herself. The little house, which had always been her haven, suddenly loomed emptily in her imagination. She whistled to Pete and, with him beside her on the seat of the pickup, took the road out of town to the Kenyons' farm.

"I'm sorry. I know I should have called," she said, pushing open the kitchen door.

"Rennie!" Sandy Kenyon looked up from a bowl of potato salad she was making. "What a wonderful surprise."

HERE'S HOW TO PLAY
"MATCH 3"

1 Detach this, your "MATCH 3" Game, & the page of stamps enclosed. Look for matching symbols among the stamps & stick all you find on your "MATCH 3" Game.

2 Successfully complete rows 1 through 3 & you will instantly & automatically qualify for a chance to win a Big Money Prize—up to a MILLION-$$$ in Lifetime Income ($33,333.33 each year for 30 years). (SEE BACK OF BOOK FOR DETAILS.)

3 Successfully complete row 4 & we will send you 4 brand-new HARLEQUIN ROMANCE® novels—for FREE! These Free Books have a cover price of $2.99 each, but they are yours to keep absolutely free. There's no catch. You're under no obligation to buy anything. We charge nothing—ZERO—for your first shipment. And you don't have to make any minimum number of purchases—not even one!

4 The fact is, thousands of Readers enjoy receiving books by mail from the Harlequin Reader Service®. They like the convenience of home delivery...they like getting the best new novels months before they're available in stores...and they love our discount prices!

5 Successfully complete row 5 &, in addition to the Free Books, we will also send you a very nice Free Surprise Gift, as extra thanks for trying our Reader Service.

6 Play the "Lucky Stars" & "Dream Car TieBreaker" Games also enclosed & you could WIN AGAIN & AGAIN because these are Bonus Prizes, all for one winner, & on top of any Cash Prize you may win!

YES! I've completed my "MATCH 3" Game. Send me any Big Money Prize to which I am entitled just as soon as winners are determined. Also send me the Free Books & Free Surprise Gift under the no-obligation-to-buy-ever terms explained above and on the back of the stamps & reply. (No purchase necessary as explained below.)

116 CIH ANWA
(U-H-R-07/94)

Name

Street Address   Apt. #

City   State   Zip Code
©1991 HARLEQUIN ENTERPRISES LTD.

NO PURCHASE NECESSARY—
ALTERNATE MEANS OF ENTRY

You can of course qualify for a chance at a Big Money Prize alone by not playing rows 4 & 5 of your "MATCH 3" Game or by hand-printing your name and address on a 3" x 5" card and sending it to: MILLION DOLLAR SWEEPSTAKES III "Match 3", P.O. Box 1867, Buffalo N.Y. 14269-1867. Limit: One entry per envelope. But why not get everything being offered! The Free Books & Surprise Gift, are after all, ALSO FREE—yours to keep & enjoy—with no obligation to buy anything, now or ever!

"But I haven't invited myself to supper," Rennie added hastily.

"No, I know you haven't. But I'm inviting you right this minute. Come and sit down. Tell me all about what you've been doing. What about the garden? I drove by the other day and it looked great."

"It is. Everything's fine." Rennie hesitated, and Sandy shot her an inquiring look. "But that isn't what I wanted to—I mean, something else has happened in my life. Well, actually, I don't know if it's happened or not. It's hard to tell, because I've never..." Rennie went to the big round table and dropped into a chair beside it.

Sandy Kenyon paused, a boiled potato in one hand, the paring knife in the other, and gave her friend a knowing look that turned into a smile.

"You've fallen in love," she said.

Rennie blushed and returned the look.

"I think maybe I have," she said in a slightly wavering voice.

"Who is it?" Sandy went back to her peeling and slicing.

"Him."

"Who?"

"Connor Blackstone."

The knife paused again, then went on working more slowly.

"Goodness, when you finally decide to do a thing, you don't fool around, do you?" Sandy grinned. Then she whirled around to face Rennie, eyes shining. "Rennie, this is wonderful!"

It was almost as if Rennie was too full of her own happiness to be by herself—she'd needed to share it. The sharing was toned down somewhat when Bob and the children came in. Sandy told them only that Rennie was doing so well with the garden and all the kids that she'd wanted to make a report. Later, Rennie knew, Sandy would tell Bob the whole story, and that was all right. At this point Rennie would have been glad to broadcast it to the whole world.

After eating they sat around the table talking lazily. Outside the children were trying to catch fireflies in the dusk. Bob said thoughtfully, "Why don't you bring all those kids out here for a picnic, Rennie? Bet they'd like a visit to a real farm."

"You mean it?"

"That's a wonderful idea!" Sandy said. "Rennie, why not? They'd love the horses, I'll bet. And we could let them have rides on Violet—she's very gentle."

"I think they'd be thrilled. There are a lot of them, though," Rennie added doubtfully. "Maybe the teenagers wouldn't be interested—they usually swim part of the day. But even with just the younger ones it's quite a group."

"And Mr. Steele and Mrs. Burgess—invite them, too," Sandy said.

"You're sure?" Rennie asked.

"Absolutely." Bob spoke with a finality that closed the subject. "You two decide on the date."

Later that evening as she headed for home with insects darting into her headlights and the lush foliage of summer bordering the road, Rennie felt a happiness as heavy and sweet as the summer night itself. She took the long way back to the city, winding along back roads she hadn't explored in years. Once she even pulled over on the grassy shoulder and turned off the engine so that she could listen to the sounds of the night—insects and tree frogs calling to her from the soft dark. Only reluctantly did she start the car again and resume the drive, heading slowly toward home. All the way she could feel Connor's arms around her, taste the sweet strength of his kiss on her lips.

She was awake before daylight the next morning.

Nine o'clock, she thought. She would see him at nine. But falling back to sleep was out of the question, so she got up and dressed in her running shorts, whistled for Pete and went for a run in the cool early morning. She watched the dawn come up and stretched all her muscles. When she returned, she fed Pete, showered and dressed and made coffee. She managed a piece of toast, too excited to think of eating anything else. Once she walked to the mirror on the back of the closet door to see if the white shorts and navy tank top she was wearing were the right thing for a day at the beach. But of course they were, and now there was nothing to do but wait and watch the minutes crawl by.

Nine o'clock came and went. Well, that meant nothing. Loading up a car and corralling a small boy took time. Still she paced and looked out the window. Finally she walked slowly down the driveway to the street and looked up and down, but there was no sign of the blue Lexus. She went back to the house.

Had he said nine? Perhaps she'd misunderstood. Perhaps he'd said ten. In any case, it would be perfectly all right to call and ask, wouldn't it? She found his number in the phone book.

"Hello?" The voice was small, a child's voice.

"Scott? This is Rennie."

"Oh, hi."

"Scott, are you and your dad about ready to leave?"

"No. We're not going." His disappointment was audible.

Rennie held the phone more tightly. She swallowed.

"We're not going? So there's been a change in plans?"

"Yeah. Dad had to go someplace on business. He had to go on some old yacht."

Though she seemed to be drowning in despair, Rennie could still react to the sorrow in Scott's voice. She struggled to keep a cheerful note.

"Well, we'll just do it another time, that's all." She thought of something. "And Scott, I have wonderful news. The Kenyons want us to come to their farm for a picnic—everyone from the garden."

"They do?" There was a faint sound of interest.

"Yes. I'll tell you about it Monday. See you."

It was all she could manage. Putting down the telephone, she walked across the room to her bed and sat on the edge of it. Despite the summer heat, she felt cold all the way through. She shivered and sank onto the bed, drew her knees up and started to sob.

What an absolute fool she'd been to think she might have a relationship with Connor Blackstone. What a silly dreamer. In the dining room of the Montgomery House she'd been very aware of those smart-looking women; she'd wondered how Connor could be happy in her company. But it wasn't women that had come between them. It was his work. He was a man of powerful ambition, of relentless drive. If it came to a choice between her and his work, then she'd be the loser every time. *Someplace on business... some old yacht.* Well, that was how deals were transacted. Rennie had no trouble visualizing the scene. Again, the smartly casual women, the men in their Ralph Lauren leisure clothes. Cocktails served by white-coated stewards. And by the time the voyage was over, agreements would have been reached, contracts signed.

Where on earth did Rennie Tate figure in such a scene? Nowhere of course.

There was a knock at the door.

Rennie jumped up, her hand flying to her hair. He'd come, after all. It was just some kind of mistake. He'd never let her down like that. Why had she ever thought he would? She must look awful. Her eyes were red, and her nose...

She dashed to the door and flung it open.

Mrs. Bridgewater stood there fanning herself with a folded newspaper.

"Morning, Rennie." The old lady gave her a concerned look. "You all right? This heat is something, isn't it? I was wondering if you could take a look at my air-conditioning unit later. That is, if you're not doing anything."

Rennie took a deep breath. "I'll get some tools and come over now," she said, hearing the bitterness in her own voice. "I'm not doing anything."

Despite her low mood, Rennie was sensible enough to realize she would never make it through the weekend if she didn't keep busy. After that one brief collapse on the bed, she refused to allow herself another moment of self-pity. She began with the window air-conditioning unit in Mrs. Bridgewater's old-fashioned high-ceilinged living room. She cleaned it thoroughly with the vacuum cleaner, changed the filter, then added fresh caulking around the unit.

"What about the one upstairs in your bedroom?" she asked.

As she checked it and repeated the procedure, she said, "You really should think about central air-conditioning in a house this size." Mrs. Bridgewater agreed to give it some thought. But the older woman was studying her, and by the time Rennie had finished, she said, "Come sit on the porch now and have some lemonade and layer cake, Rennie. Goodness, I don't want to keep you working all day. You must have plans of your own for a beautiful summer weekend like this."

"I did have," Rennie said in a tight little voice. "They fell through somewhere along the way."

"Oh, dear." Mrs. Bridgewater eyed her worriedly. "Sit and rest for a little, anyway."

"Thanks, Mrs. B., but I think I'll go work on my own unit now. I've hardly had it on this summer, and I have a feeling I'm going to be needing it today. Maybe I'll stop back later and take care of that spot in the corner where your wallpaper's peeling."

"Oh, Rennie, are you sure you want to? Well, all right, we'll save the lemonade and cake for later. But do stop and rest now and then. You shouldn't be flying around in this heat."

After she had straightened her own house and cleaned the air conditioner, Rennie turned the switch to on and listened for a moment to the smooth hum as the heavy air began to dissipate and coolness blow in. Then, gritting her teeth and pushing back thoughts that threatened to creep in, she gathered up the tools she'd be needing and went to repair Mrs. Bridgewater's wallpaper.

By late afternoon she'd done that job and retacked the carpeting on the stairs of the old house. "You could catch your toe on that and go flying some night," she scolded. Mrs. Bridgewater nodded and watched mutely as Rennie pounded with the hammer.

"Have you had any lunch?" her landlady asked severely as afternoon crept along.

"After I've finished," Rennie said. And then, remembering something, "Didn't you tell me your kitchen drain was acting sluggish?"

"Now, Rennie, honestly," the woman protested, but Rennie only said, "As long as I'm on a roll, I might as well fix it."

Hour crawled after hour, and finally the afternoon was over. Still protesting that she wasn't hungry, Rennie fended off Mrs. Bridgewater's invitation to dinner and hurried home to shower. With the water pounding down on her, tears came again, but by the time she was dry and dressed she'd beaten them back. She fed Pete, who'd spent most of the day snoozing on Mrs. Bridgewater's shady front porch. Then she sat at the kitchen table with a glass of iced tea and tried to arrange her emotions into some kind of order.

The thing to do, she told herself sternly, was to put the whole episode where it belonged—behind her. It was over, history, and whatever she'd felt about Connor was history as well. If she hadn't been so foolishly eager to believe in him, she wouldn't have gotten in so deep emotionally in the first place. Now she was paying for that. But she'd recover. It occurred to her she sounded very much like a schoolteacher lecturing her students. Well, that was probably what the situation called for. She'd certainly acted pretty immaturely.

She got up, paced the floor, looked at her watch, then whistled for Pete, and together they walked down the driveway and up the street.

It was late in the day now, and because of the weekend there was little traffic on South Street. The garden lay bathed in long shadows, green and moist looking, the plants stirring gently in the breeze that had sprung up. At the far end Mr. Steele's "horse barn" lent a comfortable bucolic look to the lot. For a long time Rennie stood gazing at it, although she didn't always see it, as thoughts kept crowding in and turning her vision inward. Pete tired of standing and lay at her feet with his nose between his paws.

"That's a thoughtful pose if I ever saw one."

Rennie started and whirled around to see Daisy Gomez at her elbow, hands thrust into the pockets of her white coat. The doctor was giving her a quizzical look.

"Just getting a breath of air," Rennie said.

"Me, too." But Daisy's dark eyes were studying Rennie. "Had anything to eat?"

"Let me see. Toast this morning."

"That's it? Lord, even I do better than that. Why don't we go over to the diner?"

Rennie hesitated, then said, "Okay. Why not?"

"If I didn't know better, I'd say you needed someone to talk to."

"Is it that obvious?"

Daisy smiled sympathetically. "To someone's who's been there it is."

They crossed the street together, with Pete following, and went into the neighborhood diner. Pete was left outside, with stern reminders not to stray, and

Rennie made sure she sat where she could keep an eye on him.

"Cheeseburgers with everything?" Daisy asked, and Rennie nodded helplessly, reminding herself that Pete would take care of the leftovers.

"Okay now," the doctor said, biting into a pickle. "What's this all about?"

Rennie paused briefly. "Mainly I guess you'd say it's about me making a terrible fool of myself."

Daisy attacked her cheeseburger. When she'd chewed and swallowed, she said, "Sounds as if there's a man involved."

Rennie nodded slowly and took a tentative bite of her own burger. "It was a case of two different worlds colliding, and I got squashed in the process."

"Write that down—good lyrics for a country-and-western song. Who was it? Anybody I'd know?"

"Connor Blackstone." Even saying his name was painful.

Her friend's expressive face registered surprise. "The big developer? The one doing the condos across the street?"

"That's the one."

The diminutive doctor chewed slowly, studying Rennie's face. "What happened?" she asked more gently.

Rennie took a deep breath. "It just seemed as if…right from the beginning we hit it off. Well, maybe not right at first, but there was something. A connection. Only I apparently took too much for granted." Briefly she told about the picnic that didn't come off. "And I feel almost as sorry for Scott as for me," she added.

"He didn't call?"

"No. Granted, I was out all evening, but even so..."

"What about your answering machine?"

"I don't have one."

"There you are. He probably tried to get you."

Rennie considered it. "He couldn't have tried very hard."

Daisy was thoughtful for a while. Presently she said, "I generally feel that if something's meant to be, it'll be. I mean, if it's right, it'll fix itself. If it's not..." She gave an expressive shrug.

Rennie smiled a one-sided smile. "This one isn't meant to be, Daisy. I know it."

"Sometimes you have to trust yourself," Daisy said. "Something similar happened to me in medical school. I fell into a pit when it was over and didn't think I'd ever find my way out, but I was determined to get my degree, so I made myself stick to it, and as it turned out, someone else came along."

"Someone who was right?"

"Oh, yes. Really right."

"I'm glad for you," Rennie said. But hearing about another person's solution did nothing to make her own heartache less painful. Still, it was comforting to be with someone as sensible and warm as Daisy—better than sitting at home with only her bleak thoughts for company.

They finished eating and Daisy said, "Got to get back to the clinic. Saturday nights we're apt to be busy. By the way, how's the woman you brought to see me?"

"Doing fine." Rennie explained about the chair.

"Great idea. Trust you to think of a good solution."

For someone else, Rennie thought bitterly. Not for herself. She wrapped in a napkin the bite of cheeseburger she'd left for Pete.

She slept badly that night and awoke early. Determined not to give in to self-pity, she went for their usual run with Pete. Later they walked to the newsstand for the Sunday paper. Mrs. Bridgewater stopped by late in the morning, in hat and white gloves and still looking concerned. She asked if Rennie would like to come along to church. Rennie's immediate reaction was to say no, but after a moment's thought she decided it might be pleasant. She'd often gone to church with the older woman, and Mrs. Bridgewater was quite uncritical about the fact that Rennie owned neither hat nor white gloves.

"Most young people don't," she'd admitted. "I just do it because it's how I was raised."

"I'll put on a skirt and be with you in a jiffy," Rennie said. And that, she thought glumly, would see her through midday. The hours stretched ahead of her, creeping like tortoises.

She sat by the window reading as evening approached, doggedly turning the pages of a new novel she'd requested from the library, one she'd looked forward to for weeks. She knew she should get up and turn on some lights; she seemed to be having trouble keeping the characters straight, and the plot kept turning fuzzy and confusing. She heard a car pull into the driveway and stop outside her door. She kept a tight hold on the book, her hands turning to ice. Pete gave a warning bark. When the urgent pounding on the door started, it took her several seconds to get up, put the book down and walk across the room.

Connor stood on the doorstep in the twilight, his light hair mussed, the collar of his knit shirt turned up haphazardly. His white cotton trousers were creased, and he wore deck shoes with no socks.

"Rennie, are you still speaking to me?"

"Of course. Why not?" To Rennie, her voice seemed to belong to someone else.

"I don't know how to begin to explain, but I did try to reach you Friday night, only you weren't home." She said nothing and he hurried on, "I know that's not an excuse, but this all came up so suddenly, you see. It was a man I'd been trying to reach. It was absolutely essential that I speak with him, and he finally returned my calls."

"I do understand, Connor."

His face looked anguished. "No, no, I'm sure you don't. And I don't blame you a bit. Only you have to believe me. It's not something I'd have done if it hadn't been very very important. I had to see him. He said if I'd drive up to Flood's Landing right away and join him on his boat we'd have plenty of time to talk."

"It really doesn't matter," Rennie whispered.

"But it does!" he protested. "Rennie, can I come in for a minute?"

She gave a small shrug and moved back. As he stepped inside he caught both her shoulders in his strong hands. When Rennie flinched he removed them at once.

"I only want to explain."

"You don't owe me any explanation."

"Of course I do!" he burst out impatiently. "I told Scott to be sure to call you first thing in the morning, but he probably didn't notice the time, or else he lost your number."

"Connor, it's okay, really it is." She made an effort to pull herself together, to keep her voice normal. "I'm sorry Scott had to be disappointed, though."

"So am I. And I know you were disappointed, too. I certainly was."

"Yes, I was. At first." She spoke deliberately.

There was silence between them for a moment.

"And then?" he asked finally.

She walked away from him into the room, turning on lamps as she went, as if the harsher light might help her hold on to reality—instead of what she yearned for in her foolish dreams.

"I don't think it pays to take these things too seriously," she said, keeping her voice offhand.

He had followed her and from right behind her asked, "What things?"

She turned, but kept distance between them, trying not to feel the pull of his powerful maleness, the emanation of heat from his body, the attraction that made her long to reach out and touch him.

"I guess I mean . . . things between men and women who are so different."

"But, Rennie, are we so different? I didn't think so the other night." His blue eyes were soft with appeal.

Rennie managed a small laugh. "Hey, wait a minute. Let's not read too much into that."

She could see his eyes darken with hurt, and for a second her resolve wavered. She'd never wanted anything as much as she wanted to walk into his arms that minute. But how could she, knowing that this would happen again, that she would always be shoved into second place behind his work? If she allowed herself to give in this time, it would only mean setting herself up for another letdown in the future. And how many of those letdowns would she experience before realizing that a truly loving relationship with this man was impossible?

He took a step toward her and without warning pulled her to him, pressing her so close she felt weak and breathless. Not meaning to, not wanting to, she leaned against his taut body, smelling sunlight and salt air on his skin, tasting the sea when his lips met hers.

"Please let me make it up to you," he murmured against her hair. "Let's drive to the beach right now. It's even more beautiful at night. We can walk in the sand and talk, and we'll forget all about this."

Carefully, slowly, she pushed away from him.

"Connor, please," she said in a tight voice. "It isn't going to work out for us. For lots of reasons."

His jaw went rigid, and a muscle in his cheek twitched.

"I can't think of even one," he said quietly.

For a long moment he studied her face as if memorizing every feature. Then quietly he turned and left.

The telephone rang, stabbing into the room's painful silence. Rennie walked over to it slowly.

"Rennie? It's Sandy. Am I interrupting something?"

"No, nothing."

There was a slight hesitation at the other end as though Rennie's mood had communicated itself across the distance between them.

"I, uh, just wanted to tell you, Bob and I have been discussing the picnic idea, and we both said, why not next Saturday? Would that suit you?"

Rennie swallowed. "Sure. That'd be wonderful."

The hesitation came again. Then, "Rennie, are you all right?"

"Yes, of course. I'm fine. Saturday sounds great, Sandy. I'll tell the kids about it tomorrow. They'll be thrilled."

"Okay. Only I know something's wrong. It's in your voice."

Rennie hesitated. "That business I told you about Friday night. I don't think it's going to work out."

"Is that it? I mean, just like that?"

"I'm afraid so."

Now the hesitation was at the other end of the line.

"Well, I'm not going to pester you about it," Sandy said. "But you know where I am if you need me."

"Thanks, Sandy. And we'll count on Saturday for the picnic."

After she hung up, Rennie stood for several minutes, not moving. Had she done the right thing letting him leave like that? But no matter how she turned it over in her mind, looking at it first one way and then another, the answer came back yes. Wearily she went to the air conditioner and turned it off, then opened a window wide. The air had cooled with the coming of darkness, and a breeze blew in on her. She stood in front of the window for a long time.

Turning restlessly in bed later, she dreamed that she was pushing through a crowd as a parade passed by. It was a noisy parade, and the bass drum thumped noisily in her ears. Ranks of marchers were pounding by, and Rennie kept nudging through the onlookers in front of her. She was searching for someone, a particular face, which kept eluding her. Each time she thought she'd spotted it, someone or something blocked her view. And all the while the noise of the bass drum grew louder, crashing in on her until she thought her eardrums would burst. Suddenly, after a roar that crackled and crashed around her, she sat up in bed. Near to her feet, Pete was whining and trembling.

Lightning split the sky and thunder pounded in great drumrolls of sound that seemed to shake the little house. The curtains at the window were billowing inward and rain was lashing into the room. Rennie jumped out of bed and ran to close the window, then hurried to the bathroom for the first towels she could lay her hands on. On her hands and knees she began mopping up the water that had puddled the floor. Slowly and cautiously, Pete slid down from the bed and came over to huddle beside her. She finished mopping and reached out to put an arm around the frightened animal, as slow silent tears coursed down her cheeks.

CHAPTER SEVEN

"NO. OF COURSE it's not ruined," Rennie said. Becky Harmon stood in front of her in tears. Around her, the rest of the gardeners drooped, glum-faced and despondent, in a sad semicircle.

The garden stretched out behind them, a sea of mud and flattened green growth. Young, just-staked tomato plants leaned drunkenly. Mud had slid into the pathways, all but obliterating them.

"But it'll never look right again," Becky sobbed. "It's not going to grow anymore."

"Nonsense," Rennie said sharply, determined to get hold of the situation before they all dissolved into wailing. "You certainly can't call yourselves farmers with an attitude like that. This is just an example of the kind of problems real farmers have to face every day. Sometimes it's bad storms, and sometimes it's no rain at all. Remember what you learned about the dust bowl out West years ago?"

"But those people had to leave their farms," practical Teddy Pohl pointed out gloomily. His Green Wonder bean lay prostrate in the mud.

"Yes, but rain isn't like that," Rennie insisted, skirting the truth slightly and avoiding mention of disastrous floods. "Everything that grows needs water. So now it's up to us to prop these plants up again, shovel out the pathways and go right on as we were.

You just wait. A couple of sunny days and our plants will be putting out new growth. This hasn't hurt them one bit, I promise. The only thing is, we're apt to get a little muddy.''

Becky swiped at her tears, leaving streaks of mud on her cheeks. "I don't mind that, as long as stuff grows again.''

"It's growing right this minute while we stand here talking," Rennie said. "Now, let's divide up and start work. We've got a wonderful cool day, and we should be able to get it all cleaned up without any trouble.''

Secretly she was feeling the same misgivings as on that first day when she'd surveyed the rubble-strewn lot. Could they really do it? On another level, however, the idea of an all-but-impossible task ahead of her was a welcome challenge. She'd awakened that morning feeling every bit as self-pitying as Becky Harmon. The thought of Connor Blackstone crashed through her head like a migraine. Arriving at the garden and seeing the sad little faces looking to her for solutions, expecting miracles, turned over some working mechanism inside Rennie. She simply couldn't mope through the day thinking of her own heartache when so many of them were depending on her. Now if she could only figure out the best way to tackle the problem. Quick tangible results were what kids needed. How was that miracle to be wrought?

Help came in the form of the Blackstone Landscaping truck, which came roaring up to the curb moments later, loaded with tools, landscaping timbers, plant stakes and bales of straw, along with Pat Blackstone, Mr. Steele and Scott.

"We were here early," Scott explained to Rennie. "When we saw the garden, Grandpa said we had to go for stuff to fix it, so that's where we've been."

"Have this place back in shape in no time," Mr. Steele said, helping Pat Blackstone unload timbers.

"Better shape than it was before," Pat said. "Scott, start handing around those plant stakes and ties. You kids can begin by staking up your own plants."

Rennie felt tears of gratitude well up in her eyes. "Thank you so much," she said.

"You didn't think we'd come this far just to give up, did you?" Mr. Steele said with mock indignation.

It was a bright clear day, and the work went well. Several teenagers arrived to survey the damage and stayed to help with the heavier jobs. Timbers were used to shore up the worst washouts. The paths were shoveled and dirt redistributed in the garden plots. Plants were tied up carefully, and Teddy Pohl announced that his Green Wonder appeared to have escaped serious damage. Rennie refused to allow Callie Burgess to do any of the hard work, but encouraged her to sit in her chair at one side and look after Donald, who was in his element creating elaborate mud pies. At one point Rennie was startled to glance that way and find the stray cat, already rounder and sleeker, snoozing in Callie's lap.

By midafternoon Rennie called a halt. They'd been working nonstop and were now mud-covered and weary, but the garden was recognizable once more—its paths cleared, the tomato plants erect again, cabbages, eggplant and peppers, looking almost better than before the storm, thanks to the straw and mulch supplied by Pat Blackstone. He and Mr. Steele were now back in the corner by the shed smoking their pipes.

"Now, what did I tell you?" Rennie said, smiling at the children as they crowded around her. "And there's more. I have some very exciting news for you." She told them about the picnic, and how they were all invited to see a real farm.

"All of us?" Teddy asked with wide eyes.

"Everyone who wants to come. I'll be telling you more about it during the week—just what the arrangements will be."

"Are there animals there?" Scott asked.

"Yes. Horses and pigs and chickens and a cow."

"Is it a real farm?"

"Of course. A small one, but real."

"Bigger than this garden?" Scott seemed fascinated by the subject.

"Oh, goodness, yes, much bigger. Quite a few acres."

"Wow."

The questions began coming thick and fast then, and Rennie finally held up her hands for quiet. "We'll talk about it again when the arrangements are made. We'd all better head for home now and the bathtub."

She'd been so distracted by their eager clamor that she hadn't noticed the blue Lexus slide up to the curb. Suddenly she heard Connor's voice behind her.

"Rennie, you should have let me know."

She whirled around, acutely conscious of the mud that hung in clumps on her heavy work shoes and smudged her face. At the sight of him the familiar painful reaction coursed through her like one of last night's lightning bolts. She clenched and unclenched her fists until she was in control again and said as calmly as she could, "Oh, hi," then added, "Let you know what?"

"About the damage to the garden. I'd have sent a couple of men over to help you. You shouldn't have tried to do it yourself."

He was his weekday business self again. The elegant suit made him look like someone she knew only slightly.

"Oh, I had plenty of help. Your dad was here early, and Mr. Steele, and then of course all the children. We managed fine by ourselves."

"Even so, it was a lot—" He broke off, his eyes full of concern for her, studying her face with that curious intensity she'd come to know.

"Hey, Dad!" Scott came running over when he caught sight of him. "Guess what! We're invited on a picnic Saturday. We're going to a farm!"

"No kidding! Hey, sport, that's great." He glanced at Rennie. "Recent development?"

"The Kenyons want the children to come," she explained. Her voice held the cool distance she would have used speaking to a stranger. And all the time she felt a twisting pain inside at the remembrance of those powerful arms around her. "They're the people who lent us the tractor."

Another memory broke in—the stubborn tractor, and Connor tossing off his coat to fix it. She hurried on. "I'm sure the kids will love it."

The cat had jumped down from Callie's lap, and Scott scooped it up to show his father.

"Dad, this is the cat I told you about—the one me and Randolph found. See how tame she is? Boy, you couldn't get near her at first."

"She looks like a real winner," Connor agreed, stroking the cat between the ears, his eyes seeking Rennie's over the boy's head.

"I was worried about her in that storm," Scott went on. "But Mr. Steele made a cat door in the shed back there, and that's where she stayed."

"Smart girl."

Scott walked off with the cat for a few last words with Randolph, and silence hung like a heavy curtain between Rennie and Connor.

"Well, I'd better be on my way," he said at last. "I have a stop to make. A small surprise for Scott actually. I bought him a bike. I'm going to give it to him tonight."

"Is it his birthday?" Rennie asked.

"No. Nothing like that. It's just...I thought he'd get a kick out of it."

And perhaps it would make up for his disappointment of last Saturday, Rennie thought.

"You disapprove?" he said, raising an eyebrow.

"It's none of my business, is it?"

"All boys like bikes," he said somewhat defensively.

"Yes, of course."

There was another moment of hesitation and then he turned away, his face slightly flushed. He walked toward his father and Mr. Steele, and paused to join them in conversation for a few minutes before leaving. He didn't look at Rennie again.

For a moment she stood there, watching as the car pulled away. All the unhappiness that she'd pushed to the back of her mind came rushing back. She could feel a heavy pounding in her head, a lonely cold feeling around her midsection. How long would it take before she could see him without reacting this way? Without hungering for him so intensely it was an actual pain? All she knew was that what was between them had shattered. And there was no fixing it, she thought wryly. Not even with a shiny new bike.

SATURDAY MORNING at nine the gardeners were lined up on the sidewalk, all of them in freshly laundered jeans or shorts, each clutching a brown paper bag containing lunch and a bathing suit. Rennie had put her foot down firmly when the Kenyons offered to feed the whole crew. "Absolutely not," she'd said firmly. "These kids really eat. And you're doing far too much already." Nevertheless Sandy insisted she would have some extra refreshments on hand. Both Mr. Steele and Callie were carrying large shopping bags which Rennie suspected contained additional treats.

Rennie's pickup would hold five—two beside her on the seat and three in a narrow jump seat behind her, with someone holding Pete. Sandy would transport the rest in the Kenyons' old van. She pulled up five minutes after Rennie, and the gardeners were sorted out and loaded aboard. Rennie went through like an airline stewardess, making a hasty count of the twelve children and two adults before they took off.

It was a bright clear day with a faint reminder in the air that September lay not too far ahead. Teddy Pohl, who'd dashed into the garden for a quick look before leaving, reported that a bean had appeared on his Green Wonder, and there were other signs of a harvest to come. Additional rows of beans, tomatoes, zucchini and cucumbers were all beginning to emerge.

Each day had been a source of excitement to the children.

Rennie, doing her best to share in their joy, had moved through the past week as though still slogging through the mud of that rain-drenched garden. She'd gone through the motions, making automatic responses and answering questions, but her heart had no longer been in it. Everything around her—the men working on the condominiums next door, Scott riding to work on his shiny new bike—had reminded her of Connor. Had she been too quick to take offense? Had she allowed her pride to spoil something that might have been wonderful? No, it was more than pride, more than a trivial hurt. It was a gulf of Grand Canyon proportions that lay between them. His friends, with whom she would never fit in, his comfortable manner in a place like the Montgomery House, private planes and limousines and cocktail parties to benefit the symphony—all were perfectly right for someone in Connor's world, but totally alien to hers. Even his interests as a developer and builder were worlds away from what Rennie saw as important to the area. Sooner or later she would be an embarrassment to him, and he, inevitably, would disappoint her, as indeed he had already. Two people had to start with some kind of firm ground under their feet, she reminded herself now.

But if her mood was a sober quiet one as they started out for the Kenyons' farm, it was almost impossible to sustain what with all the joy around her. Every young face was wreathed in smiles, and when they arrived at the farm, Bob and the two children, Marcia and Jack, were standing by the driveway, ready to greet them. Four-year-old Marcia was holding a pink piglet in her arms. When the passengers got off, she examined each of them carefully as if making an important decision, then went over to Scott and handed him the piglet.

"Hey, wow, thanks!" he exclaimed.

"Her name's Blossom," Marcia said, importantly.

It seemed to Rennie the day couldn't have gotten off to a better start.

From that moment on, there was no time to brood or regret, as the children and Pete went flying in every direction, overjoyed at the freedom of the country.

"Wait. Now wait!" Rennie protested.

Sandy only laughed and said, "Let them go. That's what we want them to do. They can't get into any trouble here."

Bob Kenyon and Mr. Steele immediately began a serious discussion of mulching and fertilizing, and Sandy showed Callie around her vegetable garden and perennial border, after which she steered her in the direction of a lawn chair in the shade of a big maple and promised to call on her if she needed an extra hand setting the picnic table.

"I'll help with that," Rennie said. So she and Sandy took charge of the table, which was laid on the other side of the same big tree, setting out plastic cups, napkins and spoons.

"I made lemonade," Sandy said, "and Bob's going to make fresh peach ice cream."

"Here's something to go with it," Callie called out, waving her shopping bag. "Homemade sugar cookies."

"Wonderful," Rennie said. "Mr. Steele's brought something, too. Let's see what it is."

Mr. Steele's contribution proved to be blueberry tarts and cinnamon buns.

"This is getting better and better," Sandy said. "You can bring this crew out anytime, Rennie."

Rennie smiled. "Wait till you've put up with us for a few hours."

In a softer voice, Sandy said, "You okay, Rennie?"

Her concern brought a sudden lump to Rennie's throat. She nodded and looked away, and Sandy didn't pursue it. Rennie, feeling some explanation was called for, said, "I'll tell you about it one day soon. Promise."

"You don't have to. Only if it would help."

Rennie nodded, blinked away tears and went on counting cups.

The morning afforded little time for introspection, however. There were horses and the cow to be marveled at, lambs to be petted. Blossom had developed an immediate attachment to Scott and when placed on the ground trotted along after him. Jack Kenyon and Donald quickly found they shared the common interests of six-year-olds, involving dirt, sticks, leaves and stones.

"Building a fort," they told Rennie when she asked, as if it should be perfectly obvious.

Then Violet, the docile mare, was led out and saddled, and each child was given a ride.

"Hey, wow," Teddy exclaimed with a broad grin. "This is really neat!"

"Toes up, heels down," Bob Kenyon instructed. "Keep the reins loose."

When Scott's turn came, he slid his feet into the stirrups easily and cantered off, back straight. Obviously he'd taken lessons in horseback riding, but Rennie was glad to see he made no mention of it and got off quietly to make way for the next rider. It seemed to her that being with the group in the garden over these past weeks had already changed him from the insecure swaggering boy she'd first met. He had, as she'd noted before, some of the natural qualities of leadership, and other kids were attracted to him. Already little Marcia was a devoted follower.

"You want to see my chicken now, Scott?" she asked shyly.

"Okay." The little girl slid her hand into his as they walked off, with the pig scuttling along behind.

By one o'clock even the wonders of farm life couldn't compete with young appetites, so everyone gathered around the table under the tree, and Sandy augmented the brown-bag lunches with bowls of fresh radishes, celery and carrot sticks, hard-boiled eggs, pickles and coleslaw.

"The idea was to save you work," Rennie scolded gently.

"Oh, don't even try to stop her," Bob said with a grin. "Once she gets up a head of steam, you might as well just let her go."

Rennie had to admit the additions disappeared in record time. Then there were Callie Burgess's cookies and Mr. Steele's homemade goodies. Sandy poured more lemonade for everyone. And it was just at the moment, when all the children were throwing themselves on the grass, full and satisfied, that the blue Lexus turned into the driveway and parked behind Rennie's pickup.

"Who..." Sandy's voice trailed off as she glanced at Rennie and saw the expression on her face.

"Hey," Scott said, looking surprised and pleased. "That's my dad."

Bob Kenyon was on his feet at once, walking over to the car. Rennie saw Connor get out and take Bob's outstretched hand.

"Hi. Connor Blackstone. Is there room for a gate-crasher at this party?"

Bob's bearded face was cordial as he introduced himself. "Yes indeed, and you're more than welcome. If you're hungry, we've got one boiled egg and a pickle left."

"Sounds like a feast."

Scott had run to join them, and Connor stood with his arm across the boy's shoulders. He looked tall and lithe beside stocky Bob Kenyon. Rennie's heart fluttered at the sight. He was wearing jeans, a navy knit shirt and well-worn running shoes.

Bob laughed and said, "Only kidding. We can do better than that for you. Come and sit down. Nobody's quite ready to move yet. How'd you find us?"

"Asked at the gas station a couple of miles back."

Sandy was already filling a plate for him.

"Sandy Kenyon," she said briskly. "And you certainly have a lunch coming. This whole project wouldn't have gotten off the ground if it hadn't been for you donating the vacant lot for the garden. Of course Rennie's persistence has to be factored in there."

"That was the chief thing," he said, smiling. "Hi, Rennie."

"Hi." Her voice was small, almost inaudible. He shook hands with Mr. Steele and Callie Burgess, and as he slid into a seat on the bench beside Rennie, she could feel waves of heat and color flooding her face.

Connor turned to Bob and Sandy. "I've heard so much about you and this farm of yours that I thought I'd like to see it for myself," he remarked. Rennie marveled at how easily he could talk to strangers.

"Not that much to see," Bob said with a wave of one hand. "We don't farm any sizable acreage, and we have only a small amount of livestock, but we do board horses."

Connor nodded with interest, protested that he really wasn't hungry, but accepted the plate Sandy pressed on him. The two men went on talking, Connor questioning and Bob answering, and presently the children stopped staring at them and went on about their games, rolling in the grass and chasing each other. One or two walked over to the fence to call to the brown-and-white cow, which stood placidly munching the sweet grass of the meadow.

"What's next on the program?" Connor asked, meeting Rennie's eyes. She looked quickly away.

"Actually I'm not the program director," she said, trying to keep her voice light. "What's next, Sandy?"

"Well, when everybody's recovered from lunch, I thought we'd take them over to the creek. Bob hung a tire from a tree branch, which I think they'll like. But then we have to get back to start making the ice cream."

"I *am* glad I came," Connor said.

Once he'd finished his lunch, Bob led Connor off to show him more of the farm. Their voices drifted back. "Well, I planted two acres of that, but I think next year I might try three. It's worked out pretty well in my crop-rotation scheme..."

Callie Burgess, still sitting at the table, pushed herself up and started clearing away cups and paper plates, and mopping up spilled lemonade with paper napkins.

"Oh, Callie, let it be," Sandy protested. "You sit and rest."

"If I sit anymore I be takin' root," Callie said with a shake of her head. "And I'm also going to walk over to that swimming hole with you. Long time since I saw one of those."

"Wonderful. How about you, Rennie?"

"Maybe. I'll see."

As she passed Rennie, Callie said in a quiet voice, "Now there's a man with patience. Forced to talk about farming when all he wants is to sit and hold your hand." She walked on by without waiting for an answer.

"Oh, Callie, honestly," Rennie said, but the old woman was already dumping trash into a plastic bag and humming to herself.

"Well, you know—" Sandy began.

But Rennie interrupted her. "Don't you start on me, too."

"Rennie, you know perfectly well that's what he came for," Sandy said. "And yes, I know it's none of my business. But maybe you ought at least to give him a chance. I mean, I don't know what went wrong between you, but are you being quite honest with yourself about how you feel?"

Rennie had no answer. She was being anything but honest, and Sandy was wise enough to see it.

"All right, Dr. Fixit," Rennie said. "I'll be nice to him."

By the time the table had been cleared, the men had returned and the children had pretty well run off the effects of lunch. Sandy herded the children inside to change into their swimsuits. Then the whole group started off across the field toward the stream.

"Dad, you're coming, aren't you?" Scott said.

"You bet I am. You go ahead, and we'll catch up with you."

Rennie's pulse was fluttering wildly, her whole body tingling with nervousness as she watched the group straggle across the meadow, Becky, the bigger boys and Pete dashing ahead, Callie Burgess and the two six-year-olds bringing up the rear, along with Sandy and Marcia, who walked hand in hand.

"What a day for all of them." Connor spoke quietly as he stood beside Rennie. "I've never seen Scott having such a good time. I have you to thank for that."

"It's really Bob and Sandy who arranged the whole thing." She kept her eyes away from him, not wanting to look at him directly.

"Yes, I know they organized the picnic. Really wonderful of them. But I mean, everything. The garden, the other kids, all the friends he's made. *That* was your doing."

"I can't imagine Scott having trouble making friends. Marcia's been tagging along after him ever since he got here. The first thing she did was hand him her pet pig."

"Now there's a love token for you." He laughed, and in spite of herself she had to join in. Some of the chill between them began to dissipate. Across the field the group had become tiny specks. Presently they disappeared into a distant line of trees.

"The stream's just behind there," Rennie said.

"Should we start after them?" He held out a hand to her, and when she took it hesitantly, shock waves of pure sensual reaction shot up her arm. The strength and warmth of his presence overwhelmed her. She definitely hadn't been honest—with Sandy or with herself—about what she really felt. And Callie, bless her heart, saying, *All he wants is to sit and hold your hand.* But that was only for today. Once he was back where he really belonged, it would be a different story. But how could she explain that? She knew it to be true, yet even Sandy would find it hard to believe her, would urge her to forget all such misgivings....

"Bob Kenyon's quite a remarkable guy," Connor said as they strolled toward the gate that opened into the meadow where the placid cow was browsing. "I didn't realize farming isn't a full-time occupation with him."

"Well, with a farm this size," Rennie said, "you'd never make enough to live on. I guess the horses they board help, but Bob's hung on to his teaching job at the college. Sandy says he really likes teaching, anyway." She could handle this, she thought, as long as they stayed on safe neutral subjects.

He dropped her hand long enough to open the gate and close it behind them, then grasped it again. Desperately Rennie hurried on, "Sandy was a teacher, too, in the school where I work. That's where I first met her. But there's so much to do here, and she's in charge of the horses. She teaches riding, too. Gives lessons to a few people—"

"Rennie." His voice cut through her chatter. Wordlessly she looked up at him for the first time. The blue eyes bored into hers as if to seek out her most hidden thoughts. "I've done a lot of thinking since the other night. How would it be if we just...started over?"

"I'm not sure—" Rennie began and then stopped short. No, she wasn't sure. Not of herself, of him, of anything.

"Maybe we were moving too fast," he said. "Maybe we should take things more slowly, start back at square one."

But there's more to it than that, she thought. She felt trapped between the wild longing she felt for this man and the doubts and misgivings that swooped in to smother her every time they were together. But longing was stronger than doubt; she supposed it always would be.

She looked at him, eyes searching, lips tremulous.

"Where exactly is square one?" she asked in a small voice.

"Right here. Today, this minute. Me wanting you so much I can hardly stand it."

She pretended sternness. "That doesn't sound like taking things more slowly."

"Well, forget I said it, then. Just believe in me."

It seemed an odd phrase, she thought. A strange way to ask for her love.

"Believe?"

"Never mind that. Let's just start over, that's all. Rennie, we all love you. Scott, my dad, the dog, all these kids, but me most of all. You're the most astonishing woman I've ever met, and I don't want to lose you. There. That's all I have to say, and if that doesn't convince you, I give up."

They paused in the middle of the field, with sweet grass, daisies and buttercups blowing around them. Rennie looked up at him. The face that had been with her every night in the dark was close to hers. She could see the tiny lines at the corners of his eyes, the uncertainty of his half-parted lips. She put up her hand and touched his cheek softly.

"I wouldn't want you to give up," she said. She could hear warning bells clanging inside her head, but distant ones, so far away that she could easily dismiss them, pretend she hadn't heard. Then his kiss overrode them, silencing them entirely, and Rennie felt her own lips clinging to his with desperation. Her body pressed close to his, molding itself to his, as she felt his strength flow into her.

"Rennie. Rennie." He repeated her name, and she could feel the warmth of his breath against her ear. She moved to find his lips again, almost as if she was dying of thirst and drinking from some pure clear stream.

Distant shouting made them draw apart. Whoops and cries and sounds of splashing floated across the field. Rennie said, "I think maybe we're expected to join them."

He was scanning her face tenderly, one hand caressing the back of her head. "All right. But let's make a date right now. I have to be away on business this week. But next Saturday we'll have our day together. We'll bring Scott so we'll have a chaperon."

She gave him a meaningful smile. "We may need one."

He bent to kiss her once more. Then, hand in hand, they ran toward the line of trees.

The wide place in the stream that formed a pool was full of splashing shouting children when they arrived. Becky was clinging to the old tire, and Rennie and Connor were just in time to see her swing wide over the pool and let go with a whoop of laughter. From the bank, Sandy kept a vigilant eye on the group. Bob was in the pool with them, his beard glistening with water. Scott and Randolph were trying to persuade a reluctant Pete to go in the water, but the little corgi refused to do anything other than stand on the bank and bark.

Sandy glanced at them as they arrived, gave a spontaneous grin and then quickly looked back at her charges. Rennie and Connor stood for a long time watching the fun, the backs of their hands touching, until Connor slowly moved his, bringing it around to hold hers.

"Okay, that's it," Bob Kenyon called at last, holding up both hands to override the chorus of protests. "If we're going to have ice cream, we'll have to start back. It's going to take a while."

"Why?" Teddy asked. "Just open a carton."

"We're going to make our own," Bob told him.

Teddy's face quirked with interest. "We are?"

"Yes, and we may have to make two batches for this crowd. We'd better get it under way."

With wails and protests, the swimmers climbed out onto the banks. Some of the smaller ones were shivering, and Connor and Rennie helped towel them off. Soon they were heading back across the field to the house.

"We're going to have to do this again," Sandy said. "Major success."

"Now there's a lady with nerves of steel," Rennie teased. She was suddenly so full of happiness that she felt self-conscious, certain that everyone must be looking at her, recognizing it. Sandy was the soul of tact, not saying a word, but Callie, more forthright, came up beside her and whispered loudly, "What I tell you?"

All the children watched with interest as Bob Kenyon set up the old-fashioned crank freezer on the back steps of the house. Teddy Pohl stood at his elbow, asking questions and observing with clinical interest. Why was the ice crushed? What did the rock salt do?

"Teddy's going to be a rocket scientist, I'm sure," Rennie whispered to Connor.

Scott, who'd gone back to the animal pens, returned just as Connor relieved Bob at the crank of the freezer.

"You know what, Dad?" His face was serious and thoughtful. "I've decided something."

"What's that, son?"

"I'm going to be a farmer."

CHAPTER EIGHT

"MAY WE BORROW your wheelbarrow, Mr. Steele?" Rennie asked. "Some of the older boys are taking a load of stuff to the nursing home. And the melons are going to be a problem."

"Help yourself," Mr. Steele said.

The garden produce was growing, not day by day, but hour by hour, or so it began to appear. Each afternoon the gardeners took home some of the bounty from their plots, but there was still a lot left over. They began taking it around the neighborhood, giving it to surprised residents, as well as to the workmen next door. Tomatoes and zucchini seemed to reproduce themselves overnight, and now the cantaloupes were ripening fast. Rennie brought part of her share to Mrs. Bridgewater. Mr. Steele made loaves of zucchini bread and distributed them. Callie Burgess brought her cucumber pickle recipe to share. Beans, bell peppers and crookneck squash began to weigh down the plants and give the garden a lush look of plenty.

Daisy Gomez walked by one day, hands thrust into the pockets of her white coat, and stopped to admire the garden. Callie promptly pressed on her a shopping bag full of tomatoes and squash, declaring that the doctor's prescription had perked her up amazingly. Daisy thanked her, but confided in Rennie later that she was sure it was the chair and umbrella that had really done the trick.

"Well, whatever it was, I'm happy for it," Rennie said.

Daisy was studying her. "And for something else, I'd say."

"What do you mean?"

"I don't see that sad look in your eyes anymore. Things take a turn for the better?"

Rennie hesitated a moment, then nodded.

Daisy gave her a wide grin. "Good. Then I can tell you my news. I'm getting married."

"Daisy! That's great!"

Suddenly the doctor looked pink and self-conscious. "I mentioned him to you that night we were in the diner."

"Yes, as I recall, you said you'd met someone wonderful, or words to that effect."

Daisy nodded.

"I'm so happy for you," Rennie said. "Be sure to bring him around."

Fred Swanson, the principal of East Side Elementary, came by one day, standing with his hands in his pockets and surveying the place with wide eyes.

"Unbelievable!" he murmured, giving a whistle under his breath.

"See? You should have taken a plot for yourself," Rennie said. "Never mind. You don't get out of here without taking home a load of stuff."

"Rennie, you're some kind of miracle worker."

"Not a bit of it. It was a lot of hard work by everyone. Mr. Steele and Mr. Blackstone—Pat, that is— saved us more than once. And the Kenyons, of course. We couldn't have managed without them."

"Well, we'll have to thank them, and we can do it at the party."

"What party?"

"I thought we'd have a celebration with everyone in the neighborhood invited. Kind of like a block party. Have to invite the mayor, I suppose."

"The kids will be pleased. Do I need to do anything?"

"Nope. I'll take care of it. You just come and bask in the glory."

"Don't think I won't," Rennie said.

"Oh, and by the way, the newspaper wants to do a story on it. A follow-up, I guess, to that first one. A reporter will be coming around. His name's Bill Darrow."

"Okay. But can't you give him the information?"

"Certainly not. You're the one who did it."

"Well, all right. Maybe it might do some good. I mean, this is an idea that could take hold, you know."

"There speaks the crusader," Fred said with his broad smile. "Now, not that I want to be a mooch, but maybe just one or two of those tomatoes...."

Sometimes Rennie found herself wandering through the days only half-aware of what was going on around her. Her own happiness dropped a curtain between her and the rest of the world. She was enclosed in a magical space just big enough to hold the thoughts, memories, words and phrases that kept running through her head. *I don't want to lose you... we all love you, me most of all... just believe in me... believe in me...* And more than words, the memory of his lips on hers, his strong arms around her, filled her mind and heart to overflowing. Some days she felt as sleek and satisfied as the cat, now named Marigold and decidedly pregnant, who grew plumper and more contented by the day, happy to lie stretched out near Callie's chair or in her lap, paws kneading ecstatically.

The week passed with maddening slowness, and on Friday Rennie asked Scott casually, "Is your dad back in town yet?"

"He'll be here tonight," the boy said, but Rennie thought he looked uneasy that she'd asked.

"Anything wrong, Scott?"

"Gosh, no. I mean, not really. It's just that . . ." He stopped and started over. "Rennie, I've got a kind of a problem."

"What is it?"

"Well, me and a couple of the guys—Randy and Ted—have something we want to do."

Rennie noted that Randolph and Teddy had become Randy and Ted.

"Something your father won't like?"

"Oh, gee, no, nothing like that. All we want to do is go fishing. And Grandpa said he'd take us. Grandpa's got this neat fishing boat with an outboard. Only we want to go tomorrow, see, and that's the day I'm supposed to be spending with you and Dad. He talked to me about it before he went out of town, and I know he's planning on it. And I mean, I want to do it and all that, only the guys want to go fishing, see."

"I see." She remembered what Connor had said about Scott coming along as their chaperon. And her reply, *We may need one*. Much as she'd come to love Scott, the idea of a whole day alone with Connor sent exciting chills up her backbone.

"Just tell him as soon as he comes home," she advised. "You may find he won't mind at all. He probably liked going fishing when he was your age."

"You think?" Scott's face grew hopeful.

"I really do."

It was ten that night when the telephone rang. Rennie, sitting in bed reading, scooped it up, feeling her heart quicken at the sound of his voice.

"You heard Scott's news, I take it?" His voice held amusement.

"I did. He was worried about disappointing you."

She could hear his low laugh. "What about you being worried? No chaperon now."

"Better be on my guard." She was holding the phone in both hands, cradling it close.

"I'll be there early."

"All right. How was your week?"

"Endless."

"Mine, too," she admitted. "You haven't said where we're going tomorrow. How do I dress?"

"Very casually."

Rennie let her breath out in a sigh of relief. Not the Montgomery House at any rate.

"I'll be ready," she said.

He was there at nine, no longer the dynamic businessman with the look of power about him. In jeans and running shoes and a yellow knit shirt he looked years younger, more vulnerable and eager to be with her. He embraced her at the door, hugging her close and kissing her until she was breathless.

"What happened to taking things slowly?" she said. But she leaned into his embrace and kissed him back, a slow lingering kiss.

"Shall we revise the day's plan and just stay here?" he murmured.

She drew back with a show of indignation. "After all those promises you made? Not on your life. What about Pete?"

"He's welcome to come."

"Good. I like the kind of places where Pete can go."

They headed down the coastal highway, with Pete stretched out on the back seat. Rennie, in her white pants and pink shirt, felt comfortable, confident and excited, with none of the apprehension she'd experienced on their first date. Was it because this was less structured, more informal? Or was it because the air was clear between them now—differences examined, misunderstandings cleared away? Something about that golden summer afternoon at the Kenyons' farm had done it, she thought. It was as if they had seen each other in a better light, and now there were no more dark places where resentments could hide.

"What about the fishing trip?" she asked. The quiet of the luxury car seemed to fold an aura of intimacy around them as they rode.

"Oh, they got off early, headed for Brisco Lake. Scott and I were making sandwiches in the kitchen before daylight." He chuckled. "Scott was afraid he'd let me down, making his own plans. I hardly dared tell him how happy I was to see him doing just that. He's never had close friends before, and now all of a sudden that's all he talks about. That and Marigold."

"Did you used to go fishing with your dad?"

"Yes, and in the same boat, believe it or not. His old eighteen-footer. The motor's been replaced, and of course the boat's been repainted countless times. But I don't dare suggest a new one."

"I know. 'They don't make boats like this anymore.'"

"His exact words."

"Am I allowed to know where we're going?"

"Cannonville."

She sat up straighter. "Really? I've been wanting to go there for ages."

"Sure you're not just saying that?"

"I never say anything I don't mean." She flashed him a smile.

His hand left the wheel briefly to steal over and cover hers. "That's what I've been hoping."

Cannonville, a historic town on the coast, had been undergoing a well-publicized face-lift for several years. Old houses had been refurbished, streetlights replaced. A new seawall had been constructed, and the town's river, the Bedford, had been enhanced with a walk and new shops. Rennie had read about the project in the newspaper, and now that it was approaching completion, she was interested in seeing it for herself.

At the end of the drive, when she stepped out of the car, her first words were, "It's great!"

They'd pulled up and parked in a visitors' lot near the river, and because it was still early in the day, they had the place largely to themselves. With Pete nosing along behind them, they explored the new walk along the river, stopped to look at the ancient live oaks hanging down close to the water and peered into the windows of the small shops. They branched out farther then, turning into residential streets and gazing with admiration at historic old houses, walking up one side and down the other, pointing at handsome doors and peering behind fences for a better look at half-hidden gardens.

By lunchtime they were ready for a break, so they retraced their steps to the river walk, now much busier with tourists and shoppers, and found a restaurant with outside tables overlooking the water. But first Pete had to be left in the car, which was well shaded by one of the old trees. Rennie gave him water and dog biscuits she'd brought and promised to be back soon.

Then they sat at an outdoor table, their hands touching, watching the strollers and admiring the view.

"Well, it's just amazing, that's all I can say." Rennie nodded. "This place had really fallen into a pit."

"The shrimping industry's made a good comeback, that's one thing," Connor said. "And they've made a pitch for the tourists and pulled it off."

"Someone must have believed in it."

"Someone like you, I'll bet," he teased. "Although I'm not sure there are any more like you."

She gave him a stern look. "Just how do I take that?"

"Everything I say about you should be taken as a compliment. Only you do have a way of tearing into things single-handedly."

"Sometimes somebody has to," she said, pushing back a faint feeling of hurt that he still saw her as an immature crusader.

"Well, you're certainly on a roll. That garden of yours is a major success."

"That's a joint effort."

He leaned toward her over the table. "Take some of the credit—you deserve it."

She looked down quickly because the sight of those blue eyes fixed on her was unnerving, and after a moment she said, "What are we doing after lunch?"

"Bikes," he said. "I saw a rental place. We can take them down to where the river meets the sea and then...wherever we want to go."

"I'll need one with a basket."

"We can manage that."

Pete disdained the basket at first, preferring to trot along behind them, but presently his tongue began to hang out and his breathing grew heavier. Connor lifted him into the basket, and he was content to take in the rest of the ride with his head sticking out just enough to see everything.

When they finally returned to the bike-rental shop, Rennie felt regret that the afternoon was so far gone, but also a firm conviction that she couldn't have pedaled one more block.

"And I thought I was in shape," she said, grimacing slightly.

He let his eyes skim over her. "You're in the most beautiful shape imaginable."

She smiled and put Pete on the ground. "No excuse for him, either. I have him out running every morning."

"Well, sometimes everybody needs an excuse to goof off. Look at us today."

"It was wonderful," she said. "This was a really great idea of yours."

"I have any number of others," he said, looking at her.

They spoke little on the ride home. Late-afternoon traffic had picked up, and Connor had to give his attention to driving. Sitting beside him, Rennie once again felt that intoxicating contentment, that feeling of being wrapped in something soft and wonderful. Occasionally they exchanged a word or pointed at a tree or house along the way, then settled back into the quiet enjoyment of simply being together.

"I think Pete's done in," Connor said as they turned into her driveway. "Do you want to feed him before we take off?"

"Take off for where?" She'd been dreading the prospect of parting from him. "Don't you want to come in for a while?"

"Hey, this date isn't over yet. No questions. Just feed your dog and come on."

She followed his instructions, only taking time out to brush her hair and apply a touch of lipstick. She could see that the sun had put patches of pink on her cheekbones and nose. When she came out, Pete had cleaned his supper dish and was already stretched out and sleeping on the floor.

"We'll leave him home this time," she said. "I don't think he'll even know we're gone."

Connor was watching her, a smile curving his lips.

"You look absolutely adorable, you know that?" Without warning, he bent and kissed her. Rennie, sun-warmed and languorous, felt herself dissolve against him and open her lips to his.

"This wasn't— I mean we weren't supposed to—" she said, gasping a little as they parted.

"No. Absolutely right," he said, still smiling at her. "Come on now. Time to think about dinner."

"Where's that to be?" she asked. "I mean, I'm not really dressed."

"My house," he said.

A mixture of emotions caught at Rennie, whirling her around and confusing her. This could be danger-ous, was her first thought. It was all going too fast. She longed to see his house, to be able to picture him in it, but there was a powerful intimacy in such a situation. Would she be able to handle it? And did she really want to handle it? Wasn't sinking into his arms and giving herself to him the thing she wanted most in the world? No. Absolutely not. He was a man she'd only started to know, a man from a world far from hers.

"Why such a serious frown?" he asked softly.

She managed a smile and said, "I think it indicates a serious hunger, that's all."

"Good. Let's go then. Scott should be back by now, and who knows? We may have fish to deal with."

Rennie could have wept with relief. Of course. Scott would be returning, and he would provide the buffer that would keep the evening on a safe plane. Sighing contentedly, she slid back into the car.

Berkeley Street was a street of old houses. All the homes were early nineteenth century, and all had been brought back to life with what was obviously loving care. Elegance and understatement were the hallmarks of the neighborhood. Dignified front doors with brass kick plates and knockers, black or dark green shutters against white siding, wrought-iron fences, flagstone walks, small exquisite gardens. Tasteful, Rennie thought. And expensive.

"Did you do all this?"

He turned into the drive of a house halfway down the block. White, like the others, with an iron fence. Toward the back, only half-hidden, a basketball hoop.

"Yes. They were all in danger of being pulled down. Some of them were multiple dwellings, some rooming houses. I saw them as part of the town's architectural treasures. I just didn't want it to happen. So I fixed them up and sold them."

"What an accomplishment," she said, and meant it, thinking how modestly he had described what must have been an enormous undertaking. He'd already done so much to improve the city. How unfair of her to have picked on him for not doing more. To have criticized the condominiums the way she had. She shook her head. Of course the people who would be living there would need the adjoining lot for a place to park. It was just that South Street was *her* neighborhood, and she remembered it the way it used to be. But sometimes towns had to change to survive. That was only common sense.

"Well, this is it," he said. "Come on, I'll show you around."

"You first," she said, letting him precede her into the house.

Her initial impression was of light. Late-afternoon sunlight streamed in, rosy and golden, from big double windows that reached almost to the floor. Despite the fact that there were houses on both sides, there was no view of them. Careful planting of shrubs and trees gave the yard privacy. Inside, the furnishings that Rennie had somehow expected to be elegant and decorator-perfect, were comfortably worn, even slightly shabby, as though they were well used and well loved. Everything appeared to have been selected for usefulness rather than effect. Couches were deep, tables sturdy, chairs inviting. Bookshelves lined one wall and more books were piled haphazardly on a coffee table. Nothing had been done to straighten the old wideboard floors, which, after a hundred and fifty years, dipped unexpectedly here and there.

"Oh, I love it!" Rennie exclaimed.

"I'm glad," he said softly, watching her. "Here's the dining room. Not used much at present, but a dining-room table's a good place for a boy to do his homework, I figure, so it may serve a purpose yet."

Rennie put a hand on the mantel. "And fireplaces in all the rooms. Heavenly."

"Well, nearly every room. Come and see the kitchen."

He led the way through the dining room and into the kitchen. Here the high-tech efficiency of modern planning was wedded to the homey look of the last century. Wooden cupboards and counters, a tile floor in a soft rosy red, a round table with a homespun tablecloth. And blending inconspicuously with all of it were modern range, wall oven, microwave, refrigerator. A huge wooden bowl on one counter held squash, tomatoes, eggplant. Connor nodded toward it.

"That's the latest load Scott brought home. We're eating as fast as we can." He glanced around. "Where is he, anyway? Not back yet, I guess."

Rennie stood in the middle of the room, turning slowly to take it all in.

"I love your house, Connor. It's absolutely... right."

"I hoped you would." He stood behind her, his hands on her shoulders. Slowly he turned her around to face him, pulled her close and leaned over to kiss her, a long slow kiss that held them together in the soft light of a day that was nearly ended. When they pulled away from each other, they still lingered, reluctant to let the moment slip away.

Can this be me? Rennie asked herself. *Have I ever been this happy?*

"Okay then, much as I regret it, I'm afraid cooking does involve a certain amount of preparation," he said. He held her face between his hands and gave her a last quick kiss. "Let's see what we have here."

He turned to the counter and for the first time both of them noticed a scrap of paper tucked partway under the wooden bowl.

He picked it up. "Note from Scott. He's already back, then. Let's see. 'Dear Dad, I caught two bass. Grandpa took a picture of them so I can show you because we're going to eat them. We're all going to sleep on Grandpa's porch tonight. If that's okay with you. Love, Scott.'"

Something leapt inside Rennie, a kind of fearful joy at the prospect of being alone with Connor in his house. All her apprehension had centered on the certainty that they were moving too fast, that they knew each other too little. Now, without the presence of Scott...

But Connor merely put the note down and said, "Well, it sounds as if the fishing was good, but I guess we're not going to be able to sample it." He was already sorting through the vegetables, picking out eggplant and zucchini, then moving to the refrigerator and bringing out a chicken. The moment was bridged. Rennie's anxiety began to fade.

"I remember doing exactly that same thing when I was his age," Connor said. "Sleeping on the screened porch was a big deal. My dad's place is out in the country on Six Mile Road. You know where it is?"

She nodded. "It's a wonderful-looking old place. I've been past it."

"We'll go out sometime for a visit. Dad loves company."

He was cutting up an eggplant with quick sure strokes, then salting the slices and putting them in a colander. "It's been really good for him having Scott here. After Mother died it was hard for him to adjust. That's when I urged him to start up his business again. Just small-scale stuff—nothing like his old company. He did really big jobs then, had crews of men working on commercial projects, landscaping for public buildings, banks, all that. Now it's just a matter of taking care of his greenhouse and once in a while doing a little garden job for a private house. He loves it."

"I don't know what would have become of our garden without him."

He considered the zucchini, selected two and began slicing them.

"What can I do to help?" she asked.

"There's white wine chilling in the refrigerator. Why don't you pour us some and then see if you can locate the CD player in the other room and put on something you like."

She did as he suggested, and when she returned to the kitchen, soft music followed her. She handed him a glass of wine, noticing that the zucchini was already being sautéed in a big pan while he sliced onions and green peppers. He worked with a casual proficiency that suggested long practice.

"You're very good at that," she said.

"I've lived alone a long time, and I got tired of eating out. I have a very pleasant woman to clean the place, and I like her to be here during the day in case Scott needs someone, but for eating I'm just as happy managing by myself. I intend to teach Scott, too. More men would be better off if they knew how to prepare a meal."

"I couldn't agree more. Which gives me an idea. Maybe I ought to run a couple of cooking classes for the kids now that they have all these vegetables to work with."

His expressive eyebrows shot up. He dumped the onions and peppers in with the zucchini. "Good thought. I imagine Dad's already showing them how to manage fish." He reached for a kettle of boiling water, pouring it quickly over four tomatoes to loosen the skins. Rennie watched, fascinated at how easily he moved, never hesitating, never making a false step. How many other men were that comfortable in a kitchen?

She sat on a high stool near the counter, her feet tucked behind one of the rungs.

"Do you suppose Scott really will be a farmer?" she asked idly.

He gave a shrug, and the movement of his shoulders under the yellow knit shirt made Rennie's stomach contract with longing.

"Who knows? At that age I think I wanted to be an airline pilot. Or possibly a policeman. I think the policeman thing lasted quite a while."

"Still . . . it could happen."

"If it does, more power to him. I'm just glad to see how much happier he is now compared to when he came here at the beginning of summer." He peeled the skins from the tomatoes deftly. "I felt so guilty at first, because I knew I'd neglected him. And I had to be careful not to be too indulgent. I know you didn't approve of the bike, by the way. That caused me some bad moments. I really trust your judgment."

She smiled at him. "I've relented a little on the bike," she said. "It didn't seem to do him any harm at all."

He put down his knife, dried his hands on a towel and picked up his wine. Leaning on the counter, he touched her glass lightly with his.

"This is wonderful, having you here," he said.

She looked up at him. "You knew I'd be happier here than in a fancy restaurant."

He gave her a long look. "Yes, I think I did." Then his expression turned impish and he added, "Of course you haven't tasted my cooking yet."

But it was perfect—like everything else about the day, it seemed to Rennie. The chicken he'd baked with lemon juice, garlic and oregano was tender and savory. The ratatouille was a symphony of colors and flavors, all its ingredients cooked just to the point of tenderness but no further. He produced a loaf of crisp French bread and poured them more wine, and they sat at a table on the back deck of the house in sight of a small garden.

"I take no credit for the garden. That's all Dad's doing."

"It's lovely, but so's the food," she said.

"Flattery, but I'll accept it."

She smiled at him. "Didn't I tell you I never say anything I don't mean?"

"Ah, I forgot. Well, then, I accept the compliment."

They finished eating as the colors faded and twilight folded around them, shadowing the corners of the garden. The sound of insects rose.

"Hear the katydids?" Rennie said. "That means summer's ending."

"Not yet, surely."

"No, but soon. It always makes me a little sad to hear them."

"But not so sad this year, I hope," he said, reaching across the table to cover her hand with his.

"Is this year different?" she asked, knowing the answer already. The touch of his hand made every nerve ending tingle.

"You know it is, don't you?" Those eyes she could never seem to evade were probing hers deeply. For a long moment she returned the look. Then very slowly she nodded.

He got up and came around the table, pulling her to her feet and turning her to face him.

"Rennie . . ." he began, but then there seemed no more need for words as he pulled her to him in the quiet shadows.

IT WAS DARK when she awoke, and for the briefest of moments she wasn't sure where she was. Then she knew, and feeling Connor's body next to her, his arm cradling her, she gave a small involuntary shiver. At once he was aware of her.

"You're cold," he said, and pulled a cover over her.

"I'm not really. Only happy."

"So am I."

She pressed her mouth against the hollow of his shoulder, feeling the pulse there. His arms folded more closely around her, and she lifted her face to his kiss. His mouth was already familiar to her, as if she had known it always. Their first lovemaking had been an exploration, a journey into the unknown, both of them surprising the other by the intensity of their reactions, the depth of their delight. And now, already, he was the most important thing in her life. She heard the words echoing in her head and wondered, could that possibly be true? But her body and all her senses told her it was.

She felt the lean length of him stretched out next to her in the bed. His hand moved along her thigh, tracing her slim waist and breasts, all the way up to her chin.

"I think I knew you'd be like this," he said.

"Like what?"

"Perfect."

"Silly. Nobody's perfect." But she loved hearing him say it. "What time do you suppose it is?"

"You're not thinking of leaving."

"No. Only wondering how much time we have left."

"How about all night? How about the rest of our lives?"

Her breath caught in a small gasp as the wonder of it struck her. He turned and glanced at the small digital clock glowing in the dark on the bedside table.

"Eleven-twenty." He pulled her close to him again. "Plenty of time for what I have in mind."

CHAPTER NINE

BILL DARROW, the reporter from the local paper, was a stocky man of forty, with slightly thinning black hair. He appeared Monday morning and introduced himself to Rennie, looked at the garden with interest and whistled.

"Wow, you've really made something of this place, didn't you?"

"The children did most of it. You'll be sure to put their names in, won't you?" Rennie said.

"Names never hurt a story," he said. He stood back and regarded the building next door, where workmen were going in and out busily. The whine of a power saw split the quiet morning air.

"Doesn't that racket bother you?"

Rennie smiled. "We've heard it all summer. We're so used to it I don't think we even notice."

"Still, if I'm going to use this..." He produced a small tape recorder.

"How about the diner across the street?" she suggested. She'd been reluctant when Fred Swanson had mentioned a story in the newspaper, but now nothing bothered her. Nothing could upset the glorious walking-on-air feeling that was with her when she awoke in the morning and stayed with her all day. Her happiness was a bottomless well. No matter how deeply she drank from it, it filled up again.

"Okay, that'll do," he agreed.

After they'd ordered coffee, Rennie asked, "Did Mr. Swanson tell you he's planning a celebration for the garden?"

"I think he mentioned it." Darrow was eyeing the doughnuts under their plastic cover on the counter. "I'll take a couple of those," he told the waitress, and while he was waiting, put his tape recorder on the table between them.

"And do be sure to mention him, too, won't you?" Rennie said. "Frederic without a *k*. He helped so much to get the garden started."

"Will do. We'll be sending a photographer to get some pictures, too, if that's all right."

"I suppose."

The waitress appeared with two sugary doughnuts, which Darrow attacked at once.

"Now," he said between bites, "let's get to a few questions. First, how has this garden project benefited the children?"

Rennie took a sip of coffee. "Oh, in many ways. They've learned responsibility, promptness. They've learned what fun hard work can be. They're terribly proud of what they've accomplished. They help each other now—that's another thing they've learned. Unfortunately we're going to lose the lot this fall, but of course I understand how necessary parking for the new condominiums is. It can't be helped."

"Those condos—what do you think of them?"

Rennie gave a little laugh. "Well, Connor Blackstone has his ideas and I have mine." She felt an inward shiver of delight when she realized how little any of that mattered. Even talking about Connor filled her with joy. "But every project he's ever undertaken has been tastefully done and upgrades the neighborhood. I'm sure they'll be a wonderful addition to South Street."

Darrow started on the second doughnut. "What do you mean—he has his ideas and you have yours?"

"Oh, I grew up around here, so at first I thought it would be nice to see the bakery back again. Pure nostalgia, I suppose. But some things simply aren't practical, I know that. I just feel the neighborhood needs an economic center to support it. Since that doesn't seem feasible, having the building done over so beautifully and having it occupied—that's certainly better than leaving it empty. And Mr. Blackstone does these things so well."

Bill Darrow reached for a paper napkin. "What kind of things have you learned from working here all summer?"

Rennie gave it some thought. "The response to the garden has been wonderful. Overwhelming. It's done a lot for the dignity and self-worth of the adults, too, you know, not just the kids. I mean, these people had their living taken away from them when the bakery closed, but they've adapted. Most of them have to commute longer distances now, which is unfortunate. But the garden's done a lot for all of them. Working in the soil does something for people's souls," she added a little self-consciously.

"Certainly the results are spectacular," Darrow agreed. He paused and drank some coffee. Then he asked idly, "What kind of force or influence in the community would you say a person like Connor Blackstone is?" When he saw her puzzled look he added, "I mean, he did contribute the land for the garden."

"Oh, yes, and we were most grateful for it." But how could she describe him? How could she say what she really felt about him when her heart was so full of love that anything she said would sound like idiotic drivel? She thought about it and chose her words carefully.

"I've never known anybody quite like Connor Blackstone," she said slowly. "He's very directed, very intense. He always seems to know what he wants and then drives hard to get it. To many people the development of a city—the way it grows—would represent a power thing. Personal gain and acquiring control over other people. But with Mr. Blackstone it's a question of doing it right, of giving it his very best. I think he always does that. And I know how much the town means to him."

She could see Bill Darrow scrutinizing her closely, and she wondered if her praise had sounded too lavish. She picked up her cup again and looked away from him, certain that what she felt must be written in every feature. But the reporter said only, "Well, good. Now tell me a little bit about what you've got growing out there, and then I'll tack on all the names of those kids you want mentioned...."

SHE WAS RIFLING through her closet that evening, looking to see what clothes needed attention, when the phone rang.

"Let me guess what you're doing." Rennie sank into a chair and let happiness flow over her in a great warm wave at the sound of Connor's voice.

"You'd get it wrong."

"Well, now, wait. Washing the dog."

"No."

"Washing your hair."

"No.

"I give up."

"I was in the closet trying to find something decent to wear to school."

"School! It's not time for school already, is it?"

"No, not quite. But I have to be there tomorrow for meetings and looking over classrooms, that sort of thing."

"Well, save some time for me. I'll be back tomorrow night."

"Back from where?" Rennie sat up straighter. "Aren't you at home?"

"Now use your head. If I were home, I'd be with you, wouldn't I? I'm in New York."

"New York!" The distance suddenly seemed immeasurable.

"Yes, but I'll be back tomorrow. My pilot's filed a flight plan for—wait a minute, let me look. It gets us in around seven. See you then."

Rennie was glad to be spending the next day at school. It was becoming harder and harder to be away from him, and she found herself daydreaming at unexpected times, kneeling in the garden to pull weeds from around the pumpkins and suddenly reliving the wonder of his arms around her in the night, his nearness and love. School would be a discipline, a focus for her attention. And it would be good to see all her colleagues again, too.

She stopped by the garden on her way to school the next morning, but only a few gardeners were there. There was less to do now, mostly just picking the vegetables. Callie, sitting in her umbrella-chair, remarked that some of the kids had been taken shopping for school clothes. "I'll be going with Randolph and Donald this afternoon."

"Don't forget the block party next week," Rennie called as she left.

East Side Elementary had the unmistakable smell of the beginning of a new school year. Fresh varnish, new books, new pencils and erasers. Rennie breathed it in happily, and this year her happiness had a double edge. She greeted the other teachers delightedly, listened to their accounts of a summer spent in the Canadian West, backpacking through France, exploring England on a shoestring. She exclaimed, laughed, enjoyed it all, her own heart too full of joy to allow for even a tinge of envy.

"Rennie, we heard what a marvelous success your garden project was. And that tan could just as well have come from the Italian Riviera. You look super," one of them said.

"I feel super," was all she answered.

The day was full, crowded with meetings and reunions. In her own sixth-grade room Rennie counted books, checked supplies, made a note to bring some plants from home for the windowsills. But at the end of the afternoon, when several teachers invited her to join them for dinner, she shook her head.

"Sorry, I have a date," she said. "Another time."

She jumped into her pickup and hurried home, where she fed Pete and then took him out to the small patio, lavishing him with extra attention to show that she had missed him.

"I let him out at noon and had a chat with him," Mrs. Bridgewater called from her porch, and Rennie waved her thanks. Finally she went in and made herself a sandwich, knowing she was too excited to eat anything else. Her ear was waiting for the sound of the telephone, and when it came she flew to pick it up.

"Rennie? Good day today, wasn't it?"

Her heart plummeted as she recognized Fred Swanson's calm voice, but she tried to hide her disappointment.

"Oh, hi, Fred. Yes. I loved seeing everyone again. And the school looks great."

There was a pause at the other end. "Say, Rennie," he said finally, "have you seen tonight's paper?"

She frowned. "The paper? No. I forgot to pick it up on the way home. Why?"

"Well...I just wondered. I think maybe you'd better—"

A knock at the front door sent Rennie's thoughts scattering. "Fred, someone's at the door. I'll get back to you, okay?"

She hung up and hurried to open the door, her heart pounding with sudden joy.

Connor stood there, a newspaper in his hand. He was still dressed in his business clothes, a finely tailored dark gray suit with thin stripes. His shirt collar was loosened. A lock of hair fell over his forehead. His face was dark with anger.

"Do you want to explain this?" he said coldly, thrusting the newspaper at her as he stepped inside.

Rennie, not understanding, but knowing that something was horribly wrong, took the paper from his hand. Her own hands had turned to ice. She could feel her blood draining away, lodging in a cold mass in her chest.

"Connor, what is it?"

"Read it, if you haven't already," he ordered.

She spread the paper out with trembling fingers and saw the front page. It carried a large feature story on urban renewal, and there were quotes from the mayor, along with illustrative graphs showing where tax dollars were going.

"I don't see—" she began.

"Right there. An interesting sidebar," he said. "Complete with picture."

Then Rennie saw it. A feature attached to the main story. Crusading Teacher Lambastes Local Developer, the headline read. She saw her own face looking back at her. Her breath caught painfully as she skimmed the story:

As local citizens debate heatedly about new developments in Palmer City, millionaire developer Connor Blackstone was the target of East Side Elementary teacher Rennie Tate's angry criticism. In an interview with this paper Ms. Tate, who has been the guiding spirit of South Street's municipal garden this summer, did not hesitate to bite the corporate hand that donated the lot for the garden. What the neighborhood needs, Ms. Tate said, is an economic center, something that would provide jobs for its residents. "These people had their living taken away from them," she pointed out. Scorning the new condominiums on South Street as "tastefully done," the spirited teacher left no doubt as to her own feelings regarding them. "He has his ideas and I have mine," she stated emphatically. "It would be nice to see the bakery back."

"Connor—I didn't..." Rennie stammered helplessly.

His eyes glinted dangerously as he looked at her. "Go ahead. You're just getting to the good stuff."

Rennie's eyes returned to the paper.

Ms. Tate described Blackstone as "very directed. He knows what he wants and drives hard to get it," she stated. "It's a power thing. Personal gain and acquiring control." As to the future of the garden, Ms. Tate said there's no hope for that. "We're losing the lot this fall. It's needed for parking—for the condominiums."

"But he distorted everything I said," Rennie cried. "Why would he do that? He had a tape recorder with him."

"Nothing could be distorted that much," Connor accused.

"Connor, this is not what I said. I mean, the words are there, but they're all twisted around."

"Really? Well, I'm going by what you told me yourself. You never say anything you don't mean. Wasn't that the way it went?"

Rennie drew a deep painful breath. "It was always there between us, wasn't it?" she said, bitterness thickening her voice. "We're too different ever to make it. I guess we really don't trust each other."

He gave her a long hard look, then said, "Whatever. All I can say is, you really had me fooled. I can't believe I was so wrong about you." His voice curled around her like a lash.

"Connor..." She had hardly enough breath left to speak his name, and if he heard it, he paid no attention. He turned and left without another word.

PEOPLE WHO'D SEEN the story stopped and spoke to her about it the next day. She told them flatly that she'd been misquoted and refused to discuss the matter further. Mr. Steele said angrily that she should "go after that reporter" and make the paper print a retraction. Rennie admitted she would gladly strangle Bill Darrow and was greatly tempted to confront him, but added that it would only make matters worse. All she wanted was to have it forgotten.

She went through the next few days like a sleepwalker. There was little activity at the garden, except for the children stopping daily to look at their crops and to linger for a while, reluctant to give up the companionship they'd cultivated over the summer, along with their rows of produce.

Mr. Steele's corner was a lavish palette of color. The repainted shed had flowers planted alongside it, with ferns in the shadier corner. Peppers and eggplant flourished side by side with marigolds and zinnias. Marigold, the cat, stepped daintily in and out through the little hinged door and napped contentedly in the catnip he'd planted especially for her.

The sunshine, which seemed a deeper gold now that autumn approached, gave everything a look of richness and plenty. Bees hummed lazily and birds rustled in the little trees at the edge of the lot. Ordinarily the whole scene would have delighted Rennie, but now she walked through it without seeing it, her eyes unable to see anywhere but inward, where her own misery lay cold and gray and unmoving. She'd lost

Connor—the reality of that was inescapable. He hadn't believed her, and without trust, nothing was left to them. No doubt he felt betrayed, too. But he hadn't been willing to let her explain, hadn't given her a chance. Her thoughts twisted in painful loops and circles, always coming back to the one bleak fact that never changed: it was over between them. The memory of the night she'd spent in his arms was like a knife wound to her now.

When she saw Scott at the garden he seemed subdued, almost as if he knew something had altered in a way he didn't fully understand. He came and went on his bike, and he and Randolph went about canvassing for takers for the prospective kittens. Sometimes he discussed it with Rennie. ''Mr. O'Brian at the diner says he really *needs* a cat.'' And Rennie nodded approvingly and said Mr. O'Brian was certainly a good choice. But try as she might, she was unable to summon up her old enthusiasm, and she was sure the children noticed.

On Friday night she was sitting quietly on the bench outside her house with Pete beside her, watching the shadows deepen, when she heard her telephone ring. For a moment she didn't move. She didn't want to speak to anyone. But the ringing persisted, and she finally got up and went to answer.

''Rennie? It's Pat Blackstone. Is Scott there with you?''

Rennie came instantly to attention. ''No, he isn't, Mr. Blackstone. What's wrong?''

''Well, probably nothing.'' But she could hear anxiety in his voice. ''But he was to come and stay with me tonight, and he should have been here hours ago. Connor had to go to the Wilton Hotel—some big benefit thing they're having for the library. Now it's starting to get dark, and I'm a little worried. I called Randy and Ted, but he's not with them, either."

"I'm sure he's all right," Rennie said at once, although she was starting to feel anxious.

"Oh, sure, I think so, too. Only maybe I'd better drive into town and look around."

"No, wait, Mr. Blackstone. You should stay there in case he comes. I'll go take a look. He could be with one of the other boys. I know where to find them all, and I'm sure I'll catch up with him."

"Well, okay. You let me know, won't you?"

"Of course."

After she'd hung up Rennie stood perfectly still, concentrating hard, clearing her mind of everything except Scott. Where would a boy of ten have gone? She knew he'd been quieter lately. Was he worried? Maybe. A new school year was looming, and perhaps his father had enrolled him in a private school somewhere. It could be on Scott's mind. What else might be troubling him?

Suddenly an idea came to her. She glanced outside and saw that darkness had moved in quickly. She went to the kitchen and rummaged in the drawer until she found a flashlight, grabbed her set of keys and whistled to Pete. Walking was the best idea, she decided. The garden was only a few blocks away.

There was no sign of a bike when she got there. Rennie's hopes took a nosedive, but she hurried back to the shed, anyway. A boy Scott's size could easily wiggle through the cat door. She took out her keys and unlocked the padlock on the shed. She opened the door, swinging the flashlight around. No boy and no cat, either. Disappointed, she went back outside and scanned the garden. She'd been so sure that his concern for Marigold had brought him here.

Across the lot, near the old bakery building, something glinted in the glare of a streetlight. A bike! Rennie ran silently through the rustling rows of vegetables with Pete at her heels.

The building was padlocked. She circled it, trying the windows that she could reach. All were locked. Some had plywood over them.

"Scott?" She started around the building a second time. "Scott, are you in there?"

But how could he be? There wasn't a hole or a crack anywhere for a small boy to slide through. Rennie tried to focus all her thoughts logically. A few feet away from her, Pete cocked his head to one side and let out a small whine. Rennie went to him, dropping down in a crouch and listening. From somewhere inside came a small but unmistakable meow.

Now she began searching frantically for an opening. There had to be one somewhere. The cat might have crept in before the workmen left late in the afternoon, but not Scott. It took her two more circles of the building to find it. A piece of plywood over a window had a small corner broken off. The window behind it was obviously broken, as well. It looked as if someone had enlarged the opening. Rennie tugged at it, splintering off another piece, paying no attention to slivers and cracked fingernails. Then she squeezed through into the dusty darkness. Her breathing was ragged and painful, her T-shirt damp with sweat.

"Scott?"

She heard the cat meow again. The sound seemed to come from above her head. She swung the flashlight's beam upward and saw that the subflooring

overhead was only partially finished. A rough set of
temporary steps led up to it. She headed for them with
Pete sticking close. She swung her flashlight around as
she went, lighting up piles of lumber, pipes, electrical
cable.

Suddenly she caught sight of a shape on the floor to
her left. She focused the flashlight on it, then gave a
cry and rushed to kneel beside the small limp body.

"Scott?" She said his name fearfully and reached
out to touch him, but made no attempt to alter his
position for fear of hurting him further. He was
sprawled on his back, and she could hear his shallow
breathing.

Urgency and fear slammed into her like hammer
blows. She must do something fast. Calling 911 meant
getting to a telephone, and it would take time for the
ambulance to get here. If she was lucky, she might find
Daisy Gomez down the street in her clinic.

She said firmly to Pete. "You stay here. I'll be right
back. Stay, Pete." There was no real reason to leave
the dog, but she couldn't bear to think of the boy
alone in the darkness. Then she went to one of the
locked windows that had no plywood over it, unlocked it and slid outside.

She ran all the way to the clinic, her breath coming
hard, fear making a tight knot of her stomach. A
prayerful thank-you escaped her when she saw the
lights were on. She burst inside and dashed past the
waiting patients.

"Dr. Gomez," she panted. "Is Dr. Gomez here?"

Daisy, hearing the commotion, stepped out of a
curtained examining cubicle, white coat over blue
jeans, stethoscope looped around her neck. "Rennie?" she said. When she saw Rennie's face she said

quickly to her assistant, "Take over here, will you, Ned?"

They were both panting by the time they reached the old building.

"I'll go first," Rennie said, and climbed in the window. Daisy handed her the small bag she'd brought and scrambled in after her. Pete was whining nervously where Rennie had left him. While Rennie held her flashlight on Scott, Daisy felt the boy's pulse, then removed her own smaller light from her bag and shone it into his eyes, bending over him and looking closely.

She glanced at Rennie. "Where are the boy's parents?"

"There's just his father," Rennie replied. "I know where to find him, I think. Shall I— What about an ambulance?"

"I have a phone in my bag. I'll take care of that. You get his father."

Rennie remembered something. "I walked here. I'll need a car."

The doctor reached into her pocket, then tossed Rennie a set of keys.

"Mine's parked in front of the clinic."

Rennie nodded and climbed back out through the window. Daisy hadn't asked the identity of the boy and Rennie hadn't asked how bad his injuries were. It was as if both of them knew that the thing to concentrate on was speed. Everything else could wait.

She found Daisy's little compact in front of the clinic, climbed in and turned the key with fumbling fingers. For an instant she closed her eyes, willing herself to calm down. She had to concentrate. She couldn't get into an accident.

The Wilton Hotel was no more than ten blocks
away, right in the center of town, but traffic was light,
and Rennie drove as carefully as she could. When she
got to the hotel she ignored regulations, parking
squarely in front of the regal old building in a Posi-
tively No Parking space. When an attendant bustled
out to the car she simply ignored him and dashed into
the high-ceilinged chandelier-lit lobby. A pair of trav-
elers was checking in at the front desk. A couple in
evening clothes headed toward the hotel's wide circu-
lar stairway. Rennie, panting and soaked with sweat,
paused long enough to look at the board listing the
day's events. Her eyes skimmed it frantically. Cham-
ber of Commerce, 1 p.m., Planters' Room. League of
Women Voters, 3 p.m., Chelsea Room. Formal Re-
ception and Dance, the Palmer City Library Fund, 9
p.m., Grand Ballroom.

Behind her a voice called, "Miss, I'm sorry, you
can't leave your car. *Miss!*"

Ignoring the voice, Rennie sprinted up the graceful
staircase. Guests in formal clothes were still arriving
in groups and couples. She dashed past them. At the
top she could look down the wide hall to the huge
double doors of the grand ballroom, now standing
open. The room was brilliantly lit, full of flowers.
Musicians were playing in the background. In the
doorway, greeting newcomers, Rennie saw the blond
woman she'd met in the Montgomery House, Jillian
Brooks. She was dressed in a long close-fitting white
gown, sequined from low neckline to hem, so that
light caught its tiny facets and shone brilliantly. Her
hair was swept up and knotted with regal elegance.

Rennie ran down the hall toward the ballroom, not caring that her damp T-shirt was clinging to her or that it was coated with sawdust and dirt. More sawdust clung to her hair. Trickles of sweat streaked her face.

At the door, she blurted out, "Miss Brooks—Jillian—I'm terribly sorry to intrude, but I must find Connor. Is he here?"

Jillian Brooks turned to her with a glacial look.

"Miss Tate, isn't it? The crusading little teacher?"

Rennie, ignoring her, looked past her to the huge room where guests stood in clusters talking and laughing. Some of them had grown quiet and turned toward the doorway. Suddenly she saw him, standing with a group, talking to another man. His back was to her, but she could see how tall and imposing he looked in his evening clothes. In spite of her desperate haste, she could feel her breath catch at the sight of him. His shoulders filled his coat broadly, and his slim waist and long legs made her remember with a stab of pain how well and how intimately she knew those long-muscled limbs and the feel of that body next to hers.

Sensing a change in the room's atmosphere, he stopped talking and turned to the doorway. Rennie sought his gaze as if they were the only two people in the room.

"Connor..." Her voice was husky and breathless.

Jillian Brooks's voice knifed through the quiet, sharp with cold sarcasm.

"It's your little friend, Con. What's that old joke—with friends like that, who needs enemies?"

Connor crossed to her with long strides.

"Rennie?" He was frowning. Rennie saw, in a curiously suspended moment of brilliant detail, the smoothly turned lapel, the whiteness of the dress shirt, even the strange intrusion of a small bandage circling his right hand. "What's wrong?" he asked.

"It's Scott," she said. "He's had an accident."

CHAPTER TEN

THEY RAN DOWN the elegant staircase together, neither saying a word until they reached the bottom. Then he said, "My car's in the hotel parking garage. Where's yours?"

"Right in front."

"We'll take that. Where is he?"

"At the old bakery building."

"Come on." He grabbed her hand, and they rushed out through the big double doors. At the curb, the still-agitated parking attendant retreated as Connor said, "My fault, Fred. Sorry." Then he turned to Rennie. "Keys?" She handed them to him, realizing suddenly that she was trembling with fear and fatigue and that he could see it.

"Is anyone with him?" he asked as they sped off.

"Daisy Gomez. From the clinic down the street. This is her car."

"Does she know how badly he's hurt?"

"I don't think so. He seems to have fallen."

"What happened? I thought he was at Dad's."

She looked at his tense profile as he wheeled the car around a corner. His anxiety was clear in his face.

"It was your father who called me. He was worried because Scott hadn't arrived. I thought he might have gone looking for the cat. He's been concerned about her."

"Were you the one who found him?"

"Yes."

"Did he tell you what happened?"

"He isn't, that is, he wasn't conscious."

A spasm of pain crossed Connor's features. After a moment he asked, "How the hell did he get in? How did you? That place is sealed up and padlocked every night to prevent things like this."

"There was a small opening."

They'd reached South Street. Connor pulled the car up in front of the old building. The ambulance was parked there and a small procession was already making its way out of the building, two men with a stretcher between them and Daisy Gomez walking alongside.

"He came to a few minutes ago," Daisy said at once, and they could see that the boy's head moved slightly from side to side.

"Dr. Gomez, Connor Blackstone," Rennie said hastily as Connor reached for his son's hand and walked beside the stretcher.

For a brief second Daisy gave a startled look at Connor, then at Rennie. Rennie guessed she must have read the newspaper article, although it seemed as if that had happened in another century.

"He's had a bad blow on the head, apparently. I think he fell from the second level subflooring," Daisy said. "He needs to go to the hospital for X rays."

"Were you the one who called the ambulance?" Connor asked.

"Yes. It's a good sign that he came around so quickly, Mr. Blackstone. Really it is."

Connor nodded, and Rennie's heart went out to him. He was trying so hard to hold on to hope, to stay calm. The stretcher was slid into the ambulance. Rennie, wanting to stay out of the way, hung back with Pete, hearing the voices, watching the efficient routine of trained medical workers swinging into action. All of it began to seem distant and unreal.

She heard Daisy Gomez say, "If you'll give me your family doctor's name, Mr. Blackstone, I'll get in touch with him and have him meet you at the hospital."

And Connor's reply, "That won't be necessary. Please, I'd like you to stay on the case, if you would."

Rennie heard the slight puzzled hesitation in Daisy's voice. "Of course. I'll follow you in my car."

"Dad?" Scott's voice was a thin thready sound.

Connor vaulted lightly into the ambulance. "I'm here, son. We're going to have you fixed up in no time." He turned, looked for Rennie and met her eyes. "Rennie..." She could hear the anguish in his voice. Then one of the paramedics slammed the doors, and they pulled away. Daisy Gomez was already headed toward her own car.

"The keys are in it," Rennie called after her, and Daisy waved without turning back.

When all was quiet again, Rennie went back inside the building. Someone had located a working light, and the bare bulb cast a stark glare over everything. She went to the temporary stairs and crept up them. At the top, curled in a sweatshirt tossed down by some workman, was Marigold with four tiny kittens.

Rennie shook her head. "Didn't you just give everybody a bad night, though," she murmured wearily, and reached out to stroke the cat.

She'd thought she could hardly wait to get home and fall into bed, but once there she found herself restless and wide awake. She took a shower and slipped into the roomy old T-shirt she wore for sleeping, then suddenly remembered Pat Blackstone. She hurried to the telephone.

"Mr. Blackstone? It's Rennie. Have you heard?"

"Connor called from the hospital. They've taken Scott to X Ray. I was just heading out the door when you called."

"I won't keep you, then."

"Sure want to thank you, Rennie, for all you did. Connor told me."

Rennie hesitated, swallowing hard. "Good luck, Mr. Blackstone."

She hung up, went over to the bed and pulled back the antique quilt she used as a spread. Then she lay down on the sheet, closing her eyes and trying hard to blot out all the recollections of the evening that crowded her mind. But they kept coming back—the brightly lit ballroom at the hotel, Connor in his flawless evening clothes, his anxious face as they'd driven off wildly, Scott's pitiful look as he'd lain on the dusty floor. Connor had spoken her name at the end. She knew he'd been trying to thank her, to say the correct thing, but too much enmity had come between them. Jillian Brooks's mocking voice sounded in her ears. *It's your little friend, Con.*

Rennie twisted the corner of the sheet and turned restlessly.

She drifted off to sleep once or twice before morning, but each time awoke with a start, unrested. She heard the birds starting to sing noisily in the trees. Then as the first gray light began to creep into the sky, a soft knock came at the door. Rennie crept out of bed and went over to it, opening it a cautious crack.

Connor stood there looking drawn and haggard, his evening clothes rumpled and smudged with dirt, his tie hanging loose, his collar undone. Rennie opened the door and he stepped inside wearily.

"How's Scott?" His nearness tantalized her. She longed to hold him close, to comfort him, but she forced herself to maintain an impersonal distance. There seemed no way to bridge the painful gap between them.

"Slight concussion, broken collarbone. He's going to be fine."

Rennie's breath came out in a rush. "Thank heaven!"

"I stayed with him until Dr. Gomez kicked me out. I'll be able to bring him home in a few hours."

"I'm so glad."

His eyes traced her features. "Dr. Gomez took her car, didn't she? How did you get home? Did you have to walk?"

She shook her head. "The police were there minutes after you left. One of them brought me home in a black-and-white, and one stayed to see that the building was secure. The cat's doing fine. She had four kittens, by the way. Be sure to tell Scott."

"I will."

The silence was as gray and misty as the dawn itself, without a spark of warmth. All that had happened hung between them like a thick screen. There seemed no way to work back to firm ground, where they might stand together and talk like friends again.

"I can't thank you enough," he said, still sounding like a stranger. "I mean, for acting so fast, getting the doctor there, even coming to get me."

"I probably could have telephoned," she said. "I just didn't know how long it would take to find you, and I thought— I guess I really didn't think at all."

"You did just the right thing," he said. "I'm more grateful than I can say."

She looked down to escape his eyes and noticed the bandage on his hand, now slightly grimy.

"How did you hurt your hand?"

He had taken a step out the open door. Now he paused and turned back. For a moment he hesitated. Then with his unbandaged hand he reached into his pocket and brought out a small cassette tape. "Getting this." He handed it to her.

Rennie held it in her hand, staring at it. Then she looked up at him, astonished. "You hit that man?"

He smiled wryly. "I hit the wall, actually, I was so mad and frustrated. But I think it scared him into giving me the tape." He hesitated. "It was all just as you said, everything. I can't ever tell you how sorry I am. I can only hope that someday you'll be able to forgive me."

She tried to say something, but her throat closed tight. She stood motionless in the doorway as he walked away down the drive to a waiting cab.

"BROUGHT 'EM BACK herself," Mr. Steele said with a broad grin as he held the door to the shed open to show Marigold and her kittens comfortably settled in a cardboard carton. "She carried 'em all that way, one by one. Guess that ruckus the other night made her want to get back to peace and quiet."

Rennie had already told him the story and reassured him, as well as the children, that Scott was re-

covering. Now, holding Pete's collar firmly, she shook
her head in wonder at Marigold's determination.

"She may feel it's pretty noisy around here, too,
with all that's going on."

The garden was humming with activity, even though
it was Sunday afternoon. The next day, Labor Day,
had been set for the harvest festival and block party.
But today, Fred Swanson and his wife, together with
a representative of the mayor's office and an assort-
ment of ad hoc committee members, were on hand, all
consulting lists and conferring with each other. A police officer was at the moment in consultation with
Fred about where the barricades were to be set up and
how traffic was to be redirected. Rennie, who'd been
told she would not be pressed into service, had nevertheless pitched in and helped, glad for something to
take up the hours. It would be better, she told herself,
once school had started. Then her days would be full,
and there would be only the nights to be lived through.

She longed to see Scott, to assure herself he was all
right, but the thought of entering Connor's house
again stopped her. She glanced thoughtfully at the
kittens. Then she said, "Could I leave Pete with you
for a few minutes, Mr. Steele?"

Moments later she was in her pickup with Marigold
and her family in a large basket on the seat beside her.
In the flurry of excitement they'd create, there
wouldn't be a chance for an encounter with Connor,
she reasoned. She'd be able to see Scott, and he'd be
overjoyed with the kittens.

She was relieved that it was Pat Blackstone who
opened the door to her, spreading his arms to give her
a hug and then admiring Marigold and the kittens ex-
travagantly. "Just the ticket," he said. "Give him

something to watch. He's doing fine, though—already wants to get up and start tearing around."

She saw no sign of Connor and didn't ask for him. She simply followed the older man upstairs to where Scott was sitting up in bed, one arm in a sling. Aside from being a bit pale, he looked so much himself that Rennie longed to give him a kiss, but she held back, knowing that ten-year-old boys took a dim view of such things.

"Hi, Rennie." He waved the uninjured arm. "I busted my collarbone."

"So I heard. Well, it'll soon mend. And I brought you something." She lifted the basket onto the bed and watched an ecstatic smile illuminate his whole face.

"Wow! That's neat. I found 'em that other night, you know. But then I took a step backward too fast. That's how I fell."

"I figured it was something like that."

"Are you going to leave 'em here?"

"For now, anyway. I thought you could look after them."

"Great. Dad says I can come to the party tomorrow if Dr. Gomez lets me. Maybe only for a while."

"That'll be wonderful, Scott."

She stayed for a few minutes more and then left, waving away Pat's thanks and his offer to show her to the door. He and the boy were bending over the basket and Scott's voice followed her out.

"When are they going to get some hair, Grandpa?"

She crept down the stairs quietly, thinking her visit had turned out well and she could leave without seeing Connor. At the foot of the stairs she heard sounds from the kitchen and stopped. This was silly, she told herself sternly. She had to face him sometime. She stood up straighter and squared her shoulders. Then she stepped to the kitchen door and pushed it open cautiously. He was at the counter, squeezing oranges on an electric juicer. He was back in comfortable clothes, his old jeans and a knit shirt. Rennie stood looking at him for a few seconds, her heart beating fast, before he sensed her presence and turned.

She could see the surprise in his face.

"Hey," he said softly. "I didn't realize..."

She struggled to keep her voice normal. "I just came to see Scott for a minute. He looks great."

"I'm so glad you did. That's wonderful."

Rennie managed a smile. "You may not think it's so wonderful when you see what I brought him."

Footsteps sounded on the stairs and Pat appeared.

"I've been sent for a saucer of milk," he announced, grinning at Rennie.

Connor looked from one to the other. "A saucer?" he asked, and then, as realization dawned, "Don't tell me. What a great idea."

She backed out of the doorway. "Have to run. I'm helping to organize the party for tomorrow. See you all there, okay?"

Back in the pickup, headed away from the house, she could feel tears misting her eyes, and she brushed them away hastily.

THE NEXT DAY Mrs. Bridgewater surprised Rennie by appearing on her doorstep.

"May I ride with you, Rennie?" she inquired. "Perhaps I could be of some help."

Rennie took in the neat straw hat, the white gloves, and said at once, "Sure, Mrs. Bridgewater. I didn't know you were planning to go."

"Wouldn't miss it," the old lady said.

Half the town, it seemed, had the same idea. By the time they arrived, the blocked-off street was crowded with people in a holiday mood. Bunches of balloons gave it a festive look, and a low speakers' platform had been set up, with the garden itself as a verdant background. The party goers were allowed to walk in the garden and inspect it, but Rennie saw Mr. Steele keeping a sharp eye on them to make sure everyone stuck to the paths. A photographer was taking pictures. Rennie recognized her, but saw no sign of Bill Darrow.

A large table in front of the speakers' stand bore colorful piles of produce from the garden. Rennie had agreed that any surplus might be sold at the party and the proceeds contributed to East Side Elementary's scholarship fund. Becky Harmon stood behind the table with a cigar box for the money, praising the quality of the produce as she sold it.

Rennie saw the Kenyons, all four of them, carrying balloons and eating ice-cream cones. She waved, and Mrs. Bridgewater said, "Now you just run along, dear. I'll be fine by myself."

Rennie was sure she would be, so she went to speak to the Kenyons, then spotted Daisy Gomez in the company of a tall bookish-looking man and hurried over to say hello.

"This is Carl Gresham," Daisy said, clinging to his arm and smiling happily. "Rennie Tate, my very good friend, who did all this." With her free hand she motioned toward the garden.

Carl Gresham smiled, too, and said Rennie deserved a great deal of credit. Rennie thought he had kind eyes and was glad for Daisy's happiness. But she had to put down the wave of longing that swept over her.

"Scott's doing wonderfully," Daisy said. "In fact he's here someplace. I laid down the law, said he had to stay in a chair."

"I'll find him," Rennie said, and promised to catch up with both of them later.

She found Scott sitting like a celebrity in Callie Burgess's chair, the umbrella over his head, the basket of kittens between his feet, his sling adding a touch of distinction. Randolph and Teddy were with him, along with several other children. Donald had to be restrained from touching the kittens, which Scott explained importantly was not allowed, as it upset Marigold.

"When they're bigger it'll be okay," he told Donald.

"So how about it?" Rennie heard Randolph ask. "Are you going to be able to go Wednesday or not?"

"Dr. Gomez says I probably can."

"We don't do much the first day, anyway."

"No, we just fill out stuff and get books," Teddy said.

"Mrs. Roberts won't be too bad for a teacher," Randolph said.

Rennie greeted them with a casual hi and then asked, "Did I hear you talking about going to East Side, Scott?"

"Yup," he said. "And I can because I'm just inside the district. If I'd been a block farther away, I'd have had to go to Edward Briggs Elementary."

"Pew!" Randolph and Teddy both held their noses.

Rennie left them with a wave and turned away, puzzled. She'd been so sure Scott would be attending a private school. Farther along the path, Mrs. Bridgewater and Callie Burgess, who apparently had introduced themselves, were bending over Callie's tomato plants.

"Those are really outstanding, Mrs. Burgess," Mrs. Bridgewater was saying.

"Well, you gotta be careful how you tie 'em up," Callie said. "What I like to use is an old stocking. Nice and soft, you see..."

From in the street by the platform came a small flurry of applause as the mayor appeared. Fred Swanson, spotting Rennie, motioned for her to join them, but she shook her head firmly, backing up and mingling with the crowd as the program got under way.

Fred made a genial master of ceremonies, speaking about the beginning of the garden and making complimentary remarks about Rennie, so that she blushed and was obliged to acknowledge a burst of applause. Then he said that a recent story in the local paper should be taken with more than a grain of salt, as they were all grateful to Mr. Connor Blackstone, who had donated the land for the garden and who had been "most supportive throughout."

Applause followed this, too, and Rennie's eyes skimmed the crowd, looking for him, until she realized people were turning in her direction again. She felt a hand on her elbow and whirled around to see him standing there close to her. His slow smile made her feel suddenly weak.

"Oh...hi," she said. "I didn't know you were here."

"Why aren't you up there on that platform?" he asked.

She shook her head again and turned back to the speaker. Connor's hands stole up to rest on her shoulders. Rennie could feel them there, warm and strong. Longing for him filled her like water filling an empty pitcher, climbing up and up until it threatened to spill over. She fixed her concentration firmly on the mayor, who had started to speak.

He was gratified, he said, that so many had turned out to help celebrate this happy occasion, then went on to indicate in florid phrases that he'd been in favor of the idea from the very beginning. He recalled how gratifying it had been, in his boyhood, to work in the soil.

"Running for office every minute," Connor whispered in her ear. She half turned to him, putting a finger to her lips for silence, but returning his smile in spite of herself.

"And now I am pleased to announce some exciting developments for the South Street neighborhood and for Palmer City in general," the mayor continued. "After several conferences with me and with my municipal-planning committee, Mr. Blackstone has announced a change in the direction of his plan for the old bakery building next door here. With a view to bringing more commerce into this area, Mr. Blackstone will create several shops on the lower level of the building. One of them is to be a bakery." Applause interrupted him. The mayor smiled and continued, "Not the old Home Hearth Bakery, which I'm sure we all remember fondly, but a bakery nevertheless.

There'll be other stores, as well. A pharmacy looks
fairly certain, and several more are in the discussion
stage. The apartments being built will be affordable
housing especially geared toward the needs of the
neighborhood.''

Rennie spun around to look up at Connor. This
time he turned her back firmly to face the mayor, who
went on, "Mr. Blackstone tells me that a new division
has been added to Blackstone Development, a subsid-
iary company that will create more such housing where
the need is seen to exist.''

"Connor, what is all this?'' she demanded in a low
voice, and this time he took her hand and said, "Come
on.''

They pushed through the crowd to the garden and
followed the path back to the farthest corner by Mr.
Steele's shed. He kept tight hold of her hand as they
stopped and confronted each other.

"What's this about?'' she asked. "When did it
happen? And what does it mean?''

He looked into her eyes in that searching way she'd
come to know and once again put both hands on her
shoulders.

"I think it started the very first time I saw you,
when you yelled at me about the trash. And then we
got to know each other, and you talked about things
that began to make a lot of sense to me. About the
neighborhood and the people and how it used to be.
And I started to think that expensive condos were a
pretty dumb idea for South Street, and so were trendy
boutiques and sushi bars. But I liked the idea of a
bakery of some sort—because there'd been one here
once before. Your friend Mr. Steele thought it would
work.''

"Mr. Steele?"

"He's helping me out with it. I began to put some ideas together and I decided to create a new company that would be independent of Blackstone Development."

"Why didn't you tell me?" She tilted her head so that her cheek brushed his hand.

"I know now I should have, but there was so much red tape to cut through, the city council to deal with, the planning board. For a time it was uncertain. And then it took me a while to buy the property on the other side of the bakery building."

"Why did you do that?"

"For the parking lot, of course. I couldn't take your garden away from you."

"Oh, Connor," she breathed.

"Remember the Saturday I didn't show up? I felt terrible about that, but the guy with the yacht was someone I'd been trying to make an appointment with. He owned a company that made the components for good inexpensive housing, and I just had to see him. I wanted to buy it."

Rennie, remembering words he had spoken to her, felt an ache around her heart. "You told me I should believe in you," she whispered. Then, realizing what he had just said, she asked, "You what? You *bought* the whole company?"

He nodded, grinning at her obvious astonishment.

"Have to have the tools to do the job," he said.

"You wanted me to believe in you, and I didn't," Rennie said, still feeling contrite.

"Well, I didn't believe in you either, did I? That stupid newspaper story made me blow my stack when

I should have known. Hell, it didn't even *sound* like you."

She shook her head, unable to speak.

"So now, here's what I think." He leaned down and kissed her softly. "I think we should do what we talked about out at the Kenyons' farm that day. Start over. Back to square one."

"We didn't really stick to it, did we?"

"No, but it was probably my fault."

"Well, perhaps that's what we need. To give ourselves a little more time."

"Not rush into anything."

"Yes. Exactly." She tried to sound pleased that he was being so sensible and practical.

"Wonderful. I'm glad we see it the same way."

"Oh, so am I."

There was a long pause. Rennie kept her eyes lowered, concentrating on the top button of his blue knit shirt, furious with herself because she could feel tears threatening again. When she finally looked up she was startled to see his own eyes crinkling at the corners and sparkling with hidden mischief.

"Does that mean it's too soon to ask you to marry me?" he said.

She let out a little cry and flung her arms around his neck, and this time his kiss was full of passion and promise.

Only when they heard footsteps on the path did they pull apart. Mrs. Bridgewater had removed her hat and was fanning herself with it.

"Really, the mayor does run on, doesn't he? I voted for him last election, but I'm having second thoughts about this one. Rennie, your garden is simply beautiful. Mrs. Burgess has given me her cucumber pickle recipe, too.''

Rennie brushed at her tears and smoothed her hair. "Mrs. Bridgewater, I don't believe you've met Connor Blackstone. Connor, this is my wonderful landlady."

"How do you do," Mrs. Bridgewater said. Her shrewd glance went from one to the other. "I don't at all mind the 'wonderful' part," she said dryly, "but I have a feeling that should be *former* landlady, shouldn't it?''

Rennie bit her lower lip and then smiled back at her. She could feel Connor's arm slide around her waist, firm and strong.

"Actually, that's true, Mrs. Bridgewater," she said. "Or it will be soon." Then she hastened to add, "Please be sure to let me know if you have trouble with your furnace, though."

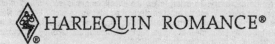

MILLION DOLLAR SWEEPSTAKES (III)

No purchase necessary. To enter, follow the directions published. Method of entry may vary. For eligibility, entries must be received no later than March 31, 1996. No liability is assumed for printing errors, lost, late or misdirected entries. Odds of winning are determined by the number of eligible entries distributed and received. Prizewinners will be determined no later than June 30, 1996.

Sweepstakes open to residents of the U.S. (except Puerto Rico), Canada, Europe and Taiwan who are 18 years of age or older. All applicable laws and regulations apply. Sweepstakes offer void wherever prohibited by law. Values of all prizes are in U.S. currency. This sweepstakes is presented by Torstar Corp., its subsidiaries and affiliates, in conjunction with book, merchandise and/or product offerings. For a copy of the Official Rules send a self-addressed, stamped envelope (WA residents need not affix return postage) to: MILLION DOLLAR SWEEPSTAKES (III) Rules, P.O. Box 4573, Blair, NE 68009, USA.

EXTRA BONUS PRIZE DRAWING

No purchase necessary. The Extra Bonus Prize will be awarded in a random drawing to be conducted no later than 5/30/96 from among all entries received. To qualify, entries must be received by 3/31/96 and comply with published directions. Drawing open to residents of the U.S. (except Puerto Rico), Canada, Europe and Taiwan who are 18 years of age or older. All applicable laws and regulations apply; offer void wherever prohibited by law. Odds of winning are dependent upon number of eligibile entries received. Prize is valued in U.S. currency. The offer is presented by Torstar Corp., its subsidiaries and affiliates in conjunction with book, merchandise and/or product offering. For a copy of the Official Rules governing this sweepstakes, send a self-addressed, stamped envelope (WA residents need not affix return postage) to: Extra Bonus Prize Drawing Rules, P.O. Box 4590, Blair, NE 68009, USA.

SWP-H794

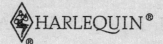

HARLEQUIN®

Weddings, Inc.

WEDDING SONG
Vicki Lewis Thompson

Kerry Muldoon has encountered more than her share of happy brides and grooms. She and her band—the Honeymooners—play at all the wedding receptions held in romantic Eternity, Massachusetts!

Kerry longs to walk down the aisle one day—with sexy recording executive Judd Roarke. But Kerry's dreams of singing stardom threaten to tear apart the fragile fabric of their union....

WEDDING SONG, available in August from Temptation, is the third book in Harlequin's new cross-line series, **WEDDINGS, INC.** Be sure to look for the fourth book, **THE WEDDING GAMBLE,** by Muriel Jensen (Harlequin American Romance #549), coming in September.

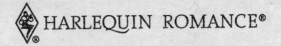

HARLEQUIN ROMANCE®

Bride of My Heart
Rebecca Winters

The third story—after *The Rancher and the Redhead* and
The Mermaid Wife—about great Nevada men and the
women who love them.

> *Bride of My Heart* is one of the most
> *romantic* stories you'll read this year.
> And one of the most *gripping*...
>
> It's got the **tension** of courtroom drama,
> the deeply felt **emotion** of a lifelong love—
> a love that has to remain secret—
> and the **excitement** of shocking and
> unexpected revelations.

Bride of My Heart is a Romance you won't put down!

Rebecca Winters has won the National Reader's Choice
Award and the *Romantic Times* Award for her
Harlequin Romance novels.

Available in August wherever Harlequin books are sold.

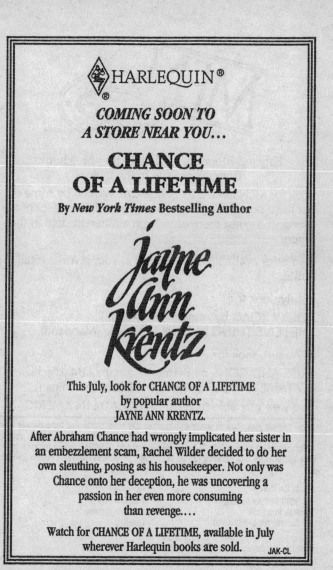

Fifty red-blooded, white-hot, true-blue hunks
from every State in the Union!

Look for MEN MADE IN AMERICA! Written by some of
our most popular authors, these stories feature fifty of the
strongest, sexiest men, each from a different state in the
union!

Two titles available every month at your favorite retail
outlet.

In July, look for:

ROCKY ROAD by Anne Stuart (Maine)
THE LOVE THING by Dixie Browning (Maryland)

In August, look for:

PROS AND CONS by Bethany Campbell (Massachusetts)
TO TAME A WOLF by Anne McAllister (Michigan)

You won't be able to resist MEN MADE IN AMERICA!